Pull up a chair... if you ain't scared.

Haints
& HOLLERS

New Ghost Tales from Appalachia

Mountain Gap
Books

mountaingapbooks.com

Messages © 2019 Deborah Marshall
Miss Vera © 2019 Brenda G'Fellers
Can Johnny Come Home with Us? © 2019 Rebecca Lynn
Strays © 2019 Brenda G'Fellers
A Visit from a Peculiar Entity © 2019 Jeanne G'Fellers
Singin' Sally © 2019 Sarah Elizabeth
Survival © 2019 Brenda G'Fellers
Born with a Veil © 2019 Jules Corriere
The Neighbors are Fantastic © 2019 Jeanne G'Fellers
Pieces and Parts © 2019 Anne G'Fellers-Mason
As Light Fades © 2019 Kristin Pearson
Great Uncle's Rocking Chair © 2019 Jeanne G'Fellers
Causing a Scene © 2019 Anne G'Fellers-Mason
The Salt Creek Valley Monkey Dog © 2019 Edward Karshner

Published 2019 by Mountain Gap Books
Jonesborough, TN
www.mountaingapbooks.com
All stories Copyright © 2019
All rights reserved
Cover Design by Jeanne G'Fellers
Paperback ISBN: 978-1-7323277-8-8
eBook ISBN: 978-1-7323277-9-5

TABLE OF CONTENTS

Dedication

To the authors included in this anthology: thanks for sharing some of your scarier bits with the world. Without your creativity and storytelling abilities, this anthology would not have happened.

Thank you,

Jeanne G'Fellers - Editor

About the Haints & Hollers Anthology

Thirteen plus one, an uprooting of tradition with another just for fun. A strong mix of history, speculation, and, perhaps, a wee bit of fear. The haints in these hills are listenin', child, so come sit a spell. You'll hear tales you ain't before; dark yahoos, wishes gone wrong, veil walkers, and someone's head might well roll. Ain't nothin' really, just a few new stories you can take back to the holler and share with you and yours. Maybe they'll shiver. Maybe you will too. And maybe, just maybe, you'll hug someone tight when things get scary enough.

Part One

. . . . ● ● ● ● ● ● ● . . . .

Short doesn't mean necessarily sweet.

(Stories Under 1500 words)

There's a grain of truth to every good story.

Messages

By Deborah Marshall

Genre: Paranormal

Keywords: haunting, ghosts, Kentucky, lost love

Fall, 1965

As long as Ellen could remember, she'd loved exploring the forest behind her family's East Kentucky mountain home. Those woods were her escape from a crowded homelife, from sisters and brothers and everything a fifteen-year-old girl wishes to avoid, but especially her older brother Ray, who loved playing jokes and jumping around corners to frighten her.

But she'd suffer no Ray today. No, this afternoon was exceptionally hot, out of place for the fall leaves, so Ellen happily retreated into the solitude and sounds of nature.

Though she'd climbed this path many times before, she saw something strange ahead, a clearing she didn't remember and... a house? It looked old, like it'd been there for decades, so why had she never seen it before?

Ellen called out several times, "Hello, the house." just in case someone was there, but when no one answered, she climbed the rotten front steps with care, overwhelmed by her curiosity.

The unlocked door jarred open when she knocked, so she peeked in before edging her way into the house. No dust. No signs of inner decay. The furnishings were old but in remarkably good condition. The wooden bench in the entrance held a crocheted afghan across its back, and a rocking chair sat in front of the parlor fireplace. Faded pictures in hand-crafted frames graced the mantel. Ellen picked up one to look closer, peering quizzically at the image of a couple in dated clothing. They seemed happy, their gaze on each other content, so much so that Ellen tucked the picture under her arm as she explored the bedrooms. When she saw nothing else of importance, she sat on one of the beds to look at the picture again. "I wonder—"

"Can you help?"

Ellen dropped the picture and fled, stumbling over her own feet as she ran nonstop until she had to catch her breath further down the mountainside. Someone clearly owned the old house, and she owed them an apology.

. . . .

"What house?" asked Sam the store clerk when Ellen went into town the following day.

"The one up in the woods, the old white house. Who owns it?"

"There was one up high in that holler when I was six or seven years old. Ed and Rose Bradley lived there, if memory serves. But the house burned during the Depression. Something about it sitting empty for a while and squatters setting the fire. I don't remember much more than that, but they did find two bodies. No one claimed them so they were buried in the potter's field right outside of town."

"When was this?" asked Ellen.

"1934 or '35."

"All right. Thanks." Ellen was now more curious than frightened by the voice she'd heard. Why had it asked for help?

. . . .

The next morning, Ellen escaped her house before anyone else woke, eating a leftover biscuit as she walked into the woods, leaves crunching beneath her feet as she sped up the path. She was torn between hoping she'd see the house and the realization that her experience might have been a dream. Neither of these suited her, but she had to know which was right.

She edged into the clearing, watching, swallowing hard when she saw the house. This had to be a different home. She'd veered off the path, gone the wrong direction... She stood on the rotted wood steps and mustered her courage. "Hello? Is anyone home?"

She knocked twice though the door was still ajar and called out again before she stepped inside, this time heading straight toward the kitchen. A woodstove stood in the room's far corner, and an empty water bucket sat on the counter alongside a metal basin. Benches and a hand-built table sat against the wall, leaving space to access the cellar door set into the floor. This wasn't uncommon for older homes. Cellars were a cool spot to keep things before there were refrigerators, but the table should've been set on top of it unless someone had just... Ellen looked up as her skin prickled. Was someone here after all?

The kitchen door softly opened while Ellen watched, and a breeze moved the curtains over the counter.

"Can you help?"

"Ray, if that's you, stop! You're giving me the willies!" Ellen spun on her heels when the breeze passed her and moved toward the door. "Ray?"

"Can you help?" No, this voice wasn't Ray at all. It was a woman's voice, soft and begging. "Please. Help us."

"Who's there?" Was this the former owner's wife? No, it didn't make any sense whatsoever. Sam had said the Bradleys' house had burned decades ago, that'd it'd sat empty before that, but..."Rose?" Ellen's voice trembled. "Is that you?"

"Help us."

"Rose?" Ellen tried to understand what was happening around her. "Are you still here?"

"In the cellar." The breeze tickled Ellen's face as it passed this time, and the kitchen door swung closed just enough that the latch caught.

How strange this was, how... Ellen followed the breeze out the door to walk to the back of the house. Ray might still be playing a cruel joke on her, so she wanted to check the cellar from a distance, from outside if she could manage it. She could imagine him hunkering in one corner of that cellar, stifling a belly laugh. She'd make a fool out of him this time by unraveling his scheme before he completed it.

Ellen found a cellar window and cleaned a spot on the glass with the hem of her skirt, looking in, pushing away with a puzzled expression on her face. There was nothing in the cellar aside from some shelves and an old wooden chest that now basked in the light Ellen's scrubbing had let in.

. . . .

The cellar felt different than the rest of the house, somehow more alive, but Ellen descended the darkened stairs carefully nonetheless. The chest sat in the cellar's center, and the tall shelves standing against one wall held home-canned vegetables, pickles, and jams.

Ellen looked at the jars, lifting a few to examine them, marveling at how fresh the contents still appeared. This couldn't be one of Ray's jokes because he'd already have had a belly ache from eating all the jam, so she set the jars aside in favor of the chest, startling when the voice she'd heard earlier spoke close to her ear.

"Please. Help us."

"I'll try." Ellen knew she was where she needed to be. There were handmade baby clothes and blankets in the chest's top half, but beneath that was a journal written in feminine script, Rose's Ellen guessed, detailing her pregnancy and how excited Ed had been to learn of it. But she'd come down sick soon after telling him, and Ed had made her stay in bed. He'd kept closed to home, tending the garden and cutting trees that would help expand their home and heat it come winter. It was easy to do such things back then, Ellen concluded as she read. Life was simpler, and the land around the house had been better cleared at some point in the past.

Ellen read on. Two weeks turned into three, turned into a month, but Rose kept to her bed, unable to hold down much, especially with Ed's horrid cooking.

Thank goodness I canned all that chicken soup last fall.

Rose's words made Ellen think of how sick her mother had been last year before her youngest sister was born, about all the pots of soup she'd made because that was all Mama could hold down

Ellen flipped through the journal pages. One month turned into two, then into three, but Ed never left Rose's side. Ellen's writing turned frail for several pages then strengthened again.

If I keep feeling better, Ed says I should be able to get back to the kitchen some, at least to cook something aside from his beans and bad cornbread.

But then the entries stopped, June 12, 1935, being the last date.

. . . .

Ellen took the journal to her mother, who first chastised her daughter for trespassing in another's home but eventually stopped to listen to her tale, following her up the mountain with the baby on her hip to where the house had once stood.

"There's nothing left but a fallen-in cellar and some charred stones." Mama sighed. "Are you certain this is where you found that journal?"

"Yes ma'am. It is." Ellen was insistent. "But there was a house here. I found the journal in a chest down in the cellar. There were baby clothes in there too."

"Well, none of it's here now." Mama shook her head. "Did Sam really say the bodies they found were buried in the old potter's field?"

"Yes, he did."

"Then we have some work to get done, girl." Mama shifted the baby higher on her hip. "We'll get started tomorrow."

. . . .

It took time and effort, but Ellen and her mother tracked down the old potter's field's records at the county courthouse and were able to search them, finding only two burials during the summer of 1935. Everyone then had believed there were squatters in the Bradley's house, that lightning had set it ablaze when those squatters were inside.

But it hadn't been squatters at all. It'd been Ed and his ailing, pregnant wife, Rose. Ellen now understood her role in these strange happenings. Rose had helped her discover the truth so she, her husband, and their unborn child could be reburied together in the family cemetery one holler over. They were finally at peace.

And the journal? Well, Ellen used that book as a springboard for a series of great stories, particularly this one, and by sharing she's keeping Rose and Ed Bradley's memory alive for generations to come.

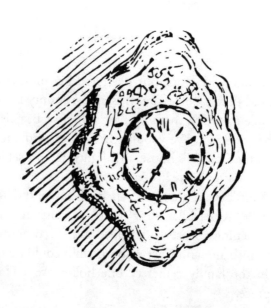

Strange things happen amid great change.

Miss Vera

By Brenda G'Fellers

Genre: Paranormal

Keywords: haunting, college, Virginia, Victorian era

A college that's about to close carries an aura of sadness, regret, and longing. Virginia Intermont exemplified this in its final days. Graduating seniors felt the weighty prospect of no reunions and no campus to visit, with diminished opportunities to connect with faculty and friends. The campus itself faced losing its usefulness after more than one hundred years of occupancy. And the faculty and staff felt a loss of camaraderie and sense of purpose.

Yet there we all were, faculty and staff alike doing our best to serve our students, to help them as needed and to see the college through to the sad ending we didn't want to face. Some students needed help finding another school. Others needed letters of reference. Still others, future teachers, needed to be certain their licensure paperwork was complete before the college closed its doors.

Like many schools with a long history, Virginia Intermont had its ghost stories, and Miss Vera's tale was the most popular. Speculation and confusion surrounded her identity, and most of us wondered if she'd existed at all. Some believed Vera had been a student who'd died tragically, and their belief was so strong that a local librarian had set out to prove Vera's identity, eventually showing that the Vera in question was indeed alive and well in the midwest.

I was an associate professor and the Director of Teacher Education during Virginia Intermont's last five years, all the way until its poignant and busy end. While I knew little about Vera's legend, I did know the Financial Aid office created a Halloween display each year that featured an image of a white-haired woman dressed in clothing from another era, sitting at a desk. They named her Vera because they believed she'd been a clerk employed by the college.

One day during March of that final semester, I crossed the

quad and entered the building everyone called Main, one of the oldest on campus. It held the Registrar and Financial Aid offices, the student dining hall, and, upstairs, a women's dormitory.

I worked with the Registrar and her assistant to change the status of a student who wouldn't have time to complete his student teaching but otherwise had sufficient credits to graduate if we changed his major. That change took a bit of time and a few forms, but we got it done. I thanked them both for their assistance, opened the office door, and stepped into the hallway.

The hallway felt different than it had when I'd entered, colder, so I looked right, toward the cafeteria door, concerned but unable to pinpoint any problem. The dark paneling told of no trouble, but still... I looked directly across the hall toward the Financial Aid office's closed door then left to where stairs led to the second floor dormitory.

A woman stood at the foot of those stairs, facing the wall to look at a clock. She wore a floor-length black dress with long sleeves, and small bits of lace decorated her collar and cuffs. Buttons paraded down the front of the dress, and a white handkerchief peeked from the cuff of the sleeve closest to me. Her hair was white and neatly piled atop her head. She crossed her arms in front of her body, tapped her foot, and turned to look at me, seeming to snort as she took in me and my pantsuit before resuming her gaze on the clock.

How pale she was, her skin paper if not narcissus white. Her face, her hands, her neck, all she dared to reveal was as white as fresh snow. She made no effort to move toward me, indeed, took no notice of me after her quick examination and snort of disdain.

I now had an answer to the mystery of Vera's identity. She'd been a housemother, either from the late 1800s or early 1900s, a late-era Victorian woman.

I suddenly felt faint, so I re-entered the Registrar's office where I sat heavily on the bench just inside the door.

"Did you forget something?" asked the assistant as she

looked up. "Oh, you're... Are you okay?"

"I just saw Vera."

Beware of spirits willing to relocate.

Can Johnny Come Home With us?

By Rebecca Lynn

Genre: Paranormal

Keywords: cemetery, haunting, Memorial Day, ghosts

Every Memorial Day morning, we follow an old Decoration Day tradition, planting flowers, scrubbing headstones of deceased loved ones, and remembering those who have gone before us. We used to picnic in the cemeteries too, but these days we have family get-togethers and barbecues instead. We've a lot to get done today in that regard, so my Aunt Carol picks us up at the crack of dawn to visit a nearly forgotten cemetery that holds several distant relatives to whom we're going to pay our respects.

As we wash the gravestones, my three-year-old daughter, Emily, plays on a blanket near the car, which is parked on the side of the overgrown dirt road that winds its way through the cemetery. She's only a few yards away, and I can hear her talking to her toys in her various make-believe voices. She and her Littlest Pet Shop figures are having a fabulous time. It's a beautiful spring morning, and the flowers we're planting in front of the graves look lovely.

I finish scrubbing the front of a headstone and move to the back, but I want to check on Emily first. To my surprise, she's gone, no longer on the blanket she knows she's supposed to stay on. I call for her, certain she's close, cupping my hands like a megaphone, but she doesn't respond.

Aunt Carol and I search frantically, and I call out until I'm hoarse and frightened enough to call the police. I pull my phone from my pocket and dial nine before I hear giggling.

"You hear that?" Aunt Carol points to a black granite gravestone surrounded by spiked, knee-high fencing. "She's hiding from us."

"How'd she get in there?" Behind the gravestone sits Emily, crouched, her hands and fingers intertwined with the air.

"Emily!" I turn off my phone and tuck it into my pocket. "You know better than to hide from Mommy and Aunt Carol.

"Johnny said it would be fun." She wiggles her fingers and grins at... I see nothing but air.

Aunt Carol and I look at each other before I answer. "He did, did he? Aren't you supposed to do what Mommy says first?"

Emily looks at the grass. "Yes, Mommy."

"Okay, then." I step over the fence to take her hand, but she pulls back and shakes her head.

"Johnny's got me; he'll help me up."

I gasp as she rises and floats over the fence, her arms outstretched with her little fingers curled as if she's holding hands with someone. Aunt Carol stares like I am, her eyes huge as she bites her bottom lip.

"Mommy?" Emily lands beside me. "Can Johnny come home with us?"

I gulp. What am I to do, to say, to..."No, honey. Johnny has to stay here."

"He lives here." Aunt Carol rushes to add.

"But he doesn't have a family," Emily sounds so sad. "He's all alone here."

"What's Johnny's last name?" I ask her. Maybe we're overreacting, Perhaps she's just playing pretend and will give us the name of one of her imaginary friends.

"Um, hold on." Emily stands on her toes to whisper to her new friend. "His name is Jonathan Michael Hertz. Johnny."

My brow wrinkles as I think on the name. Is that someone from television or from a book I've read her?

"Can he? Pleeaase, Mommy? He says he'll be good."

"No, Emily." I stare behind my daughter at the air, her friend, whatever's been talking to her. "He needs to stay here."

Aunt Carol repeats my verdict. "Say goodbye, dear. It's time to go home."

Emily cries as I carry her to the car. I'm saying prayers under my breath and then out loud as we go, hoping that's enough for Johnny, if that's his name, to get the message.

"Do you think?" Aunt Carol asks as she climbs into the driver's seat.

"Do you?" I know what she's asking, and my heart pounds when I acknowledge it. We get out of the car without saying another word, my hold on Emily frantic.

Emily waves as we near the black gravestone, and I suck in my breath. The name on the tombstone reads Jonathan Michael Hertz, died age fifteen.

"Emily can't read yet," I say. "This is creepy."

"Your mother says you did the same thing at Emily's age, so it must run in the family." Aunt Carol grabs Emily and races toward the car. "His name was Johnny!"

The hairs on my arms stand on end as I look at Johnny's gravesite. We know each other? If so, I've no memory. "We're going home now, Johnny. So stay put, right here. This is your home, okay?" I run back to the car and tell Aunt Carol to go, hoping Johnny was the only one wanting to come home with us.

This mutt and Mastiff aren't playing nice.

Strays

By Brenda G'Fellers

Genre: Paranormal

Keywords: dogs, ghosts, Kentucky, coal country, summer, sisters

CW: dog attack

It's 1959, and summer has come to the heart of coal country, making everything green. On Sandlick Road, near Whitesburg, Kentucky, just beyond a railroad crossing, stands a beautiful two-story white frame house. Next to that house there is a driveway that continues for another quarter mile, past long-abandoned chicken coops and derelict fields, and at the end of that drive sits a small rental house, four rooms, with electricity, ten dollars per month, a bargain at that price.

An outhouse stands just left of the rental house's porch. The household water comes from a creek that runs down the mountain, but the water tastes slightly bitter, the probable result of several abandoned mines that dot the surrounding area. Someone can stand or stoop on the small wooden bridge crossing the creek and fill the household water bucket, then turn and look up the hill to an old road leading to the mouth of an abandoned mine.

Of the children in our family, three of us are old enough to venture outside alone, but we're forbidden to play in or around the mine. We can play in the surrounding forest or in the weedy fields instead. There's a tree growing in one of those fields at almost a ninety-degree angle to the ground, so I can lie on its trunk and wonder what the future might bring or if my parents will argue today. This is my favorite place to be.

My younger sisters Leigh and Irene and I often explore the woods, especially those on the other side of the bridge from our house, but we often venture near the mine despite our mother's warning. The terrain isn't that steep, and there's a moss-covered, level clearing nearby. Hundreds of flat rocks hide amid the moss, so we decide to build a fort, using them for the walls.

We stack the rocks, transplanting moss to cover any bare spots. It's hot work, but we keep at it throughout the summer, working almost every sunny day unless our mother needs help.

Our landlord's daughter, Kylie, bored by midsummer, comes to see what we're doing and joins in our building, so the fort grows.

We occasionally see squirrels and rabbits around the edge of the woods, but we rarely see other animals. Four girls building and laughing together probably drove them away. Still, we build most every day we can and, by July, we have a nice fort in the making.

It's a hot day, and we're sticky and sweaty. We've reached the point in our building where we can discuss the fort's inner walls, so we're arguing about how they should go together. But we soon decide we'll draw a plan in the dirt instead. We use sticks to mark a general outline then begin working on the lines representing the interior walls.

We're deep in our planning when we hear a dog crashing and barking through the woods. We stare at each other then leap up to shelter behind our fort's walls, Kylie wielding the stick she's been drawing with, the only one stout enough to be a weapon.

A dog, a dark brindled Mastiff, walks outside our fort, sniffing then growling and barking at us. It stands at the fort's opening, and Kylie bravely raises the stick as my sisters and I cower.

The dog lifts its head and looks around, backing a few steps from Kylie. There's a yapping noise and a second dog, a mutt, rushes toward the Mastiff. This dog is much smaller, and we fear for it as it stops, looks at the fort then toward the big dog, which turns its attention to the newcomer.

The brindle snarls and advances slowly toward the little dog. "Run!" we yell, but to our surprise, the mutt leaps at the larger dog, sinking its teeth into the Mastiff's throat. This time we all shrink back, but we can't tear our eyes away.

The Mastiff shakes its head violently back and forth until it flings the mutt into the brush, but we're not safe yet, so Kylie brandishes her stick. The small dog rises as she does so, circling the Mastiff before flinging itself at its throat once again.

This time the Mastiff backs from our fort, shaking its head, the mutt holding on until it's shaken free and the bigger dog runs into the woods. The little dog picks itself up again, wagging its tail as it walks toward us.

We pour out of our fort to pet our hero, to thank it for defending us. Kylie and I extend our hands to pet our rescuer, but the little dog vanishes before our eyes. "A ghost!" Kylie shouts. "It was a ghost!"

"Was the big dog a ghost too?" I ask. "Are they locked in an ongoing fight even though they're dead?" Till this day I often overthink such things.

We gather our belongings and our trash and go to our homes, leaving our fort abandoned on the mountainside. Maybe its remains are still there. Maybe the two dogs are there too, repeating their battle. But maybe, just maybe, it was all a dream.

Here's looking at you, kid, through glowing red eyes.

A Visit From a Peculiar Entity

By Jeanne G'Fellers

Genre: Paranormal

Keywords: spirits, family, Tennessee, work

October 2009

I'm long past tired and on toward exhausted when I finish teaching my American Literature night course, and I still have an hour drive ahead of me. Day classes, night classes, a two-hour round-trip commute, so goes my life. As a parent of three children, I desperately need a job with benefits, which is why I make the commute four days a week, but on Wednesdays I remain on campus from nine a.m. until nearly ten p.m. The trip home those nights requires caffeine and a snack so I'll remain wide awake until I leave the interstate. At that point, the road becomes a wide two-lane state highway through mainly farmland, so I normally relax, but I also try to remain alert. It's well into fall, and that means white-tailed deer will cross the road before me at least once more nights than not.

This night has been no exception. I see two does leap across the road as soon as I exit the interstate, and a young buck crosses ahead of me a few miles later, this time at the last major turn off before I reach home. I only have three miles after that, so I turn up the radio and switch on my high beams, a small warning beacon to whatever might be thinking about crossing the road.

Stay out of my way. I'm tired. I've had a thirteen hour day. I... What the hell is that?

I slow to a near stop on the otherwise deserted two-lane road and squint. I know I'm exhausted. I know it's late. I probably need my eyes examined, but... I roll the minivan to a complete stop and raise my glasses to scrub my eyes with the back of my hand, but I still see... whatever it is.

To this day the best description I have for what I saw is an Ent. You remember Ents, don't you? If you've read Tolkien's *Lord of the Rings* fantasy series or watched the movies, then you know what an Ent is. They're a tree-like race of creatures, long barked bodies, leaf-covered limbs, and faces embedded on their trunks. In Tolkien's Middle Earth, the ancient Ents will talk to you and even fight, but they'd rather be left alone.

But to the best of my memory, Tolkien's Ents never glowed like a neon sign.

This creature is a black, unlit void at its center, between eight and ten feet tall, and it's crossing the road dead ahead. There's green surrounding its midnight center, and the closer to the creature's edge the green gets, the more it glows. I've no other way to describe it than as a neon-edged mini Ent, and it's casually striding across the road as if it *wants* me to see it. Maybe it does, maybe... It turns its head when it reaches the road's shoulder to stare at me with glowing red eyes before it fades from sight.

"O...kay." I'm a mile from home and scared out of my wits by something I can't well describe at the time, so I say nothing else, but I'm still shaking when I reach home.

"You all right?" my wife asks as soon as I walk into the house.

"I almost hit a deer." I drop my bag and head toward the bathroom to wash my face, staring at myself in the mirror for a good fifteen minutes afterward. What did I just see? Am I so tired I've hallucinated? What the... I decide to tell no one about the incident because if I can't believe what I've seen, then I'm certain no one else will.

. . . .

May 2019

My youngest son, Jess, the logical explanation seeker and doubter in our family, the one who refuses to address anything outside the norm, is home from college with his new wife, and we're sitting in the den swapping stories when out of the blue...

"I've never told you this because I didn't think you'd believe me." Jess shifts on the couch so he better faces me. "When I was nine or ten, I woke up one night to this weird, tree-like black and glowing green thing in my room. It filled the entire corner and had the strangest red eyes." He goes on to describe the being in fine detail, but the words "tree-like" stand out most to me.

I'm rapt because I know this story far too well, but as a parent, I'm also concerned. He was nine or ten years old when this happened, when it happened to me too, and while I had difficulty processing what I saw as an adult, I simply cannot imagine seeing it as a child. "Why didn't you call out or say anything?"

"I tried, but I couldn't! It wouldn't let me!" Jess grabs his wife's arm, visibly frightened by what he's telling me. "It kept coming closer, but no matter how I tried to scream, it wouldn't let me, so I finally closed my eyes and hoped it'd go away. Then when I finally opened my eyes, it was gone."

"Where was I?" I'm certain I was there; I was every night aside from...

"You were teaching a night course up in Kingsport. You came home soon after, but you stayed in the bathroom for such a long time that I think I finally fell asleep." He scrunches his face. "I didn't think you'd believe me anyway."

"Yeah, I would have." I tell him my side of the story, of seeing the same entity, of being too frightened to say anything about it then. Had this being wanted us not to speak about its visit? Had it instilled some sort of block so we wouldn't forget but also never speak of it? And most of all, why us? Why did it choose to show itself to us, and on the same night too?

I'm still curious a decade later, especially after what Jess shared, but I certainly don't want the Ent-ish creature to return so I can ask it face to red-eyed face.

Part Two

· · · · · · · · · ● ● ● ● ● ● ● ● · · · · ·

Here's to sad songs, rabid beasts,

and things best left unseen.

(Stories 1,500-2,500 words)

A sad, haunting lullaby.

Singin' Sally

By Sarah Elizabeth

Genre: Paranormal

Keywords: haunting, ghosts, Tennessee, camping, river, water

CW: depression, murder-suicide

Down Clark's Creek Road, at the edge of the Cherokee National Forest, on the trail head, a faded sign reads, "Overnight campers use caution. Aggressive bears in area." It keeps people away aside from the occasional daring teenager or the disbelieving passerby. But the locals know better. The sign hangs by a rusty nail that groans in anguish with each passing wind, exclaiming what the sign really means, what it really warns about, for the locals all know there haven't been bears in that part of the forest as long as anyone can remember.

It's still a drive past the rusty nail and faded sign and down a forgotten dirt road to Sally's Hole. The thick green canopy overhead blocks out the light except for the occasional sliver that sneaks in when the wind blows. There's a creek leading from that hole to the river, and over the river is the sunlit exception. No tree can reach over the unhurried water even though its berth is slight and some of the trees are mighty. They stretch and moan but will never succeed, so the land above maintains a clear view from the water to the sky, just the way Old Joe prefers it.

The nearby river is normally tepid and lazy, with a chilled undercurrent that'll send spurs up the spine of even skilled fishermen. No matter the weather, the temperature in the water leading to Sally's Hole never changes. Fish still swim the current; they still gather in the Hole, and the occasional passerby, with a guide book to best fishing, will set out to snag some trout, unaware that their catch will bear the taste of sorrow and regret. One bite of Sally's fish and every buried contrition will flood through their body, leaving their soul damp and achy. No matter how much they try to drink it down, the bitter taste of desperation will linger on their tongue and haunt them, sending singeing tears of *what if* down their face.

From the tired sign, in the opposite direction, down the gravel road and across the two-lane highway, a produce store stands and watches those who are brave or foolish enough to face the bears. There, over the corn and pumpkins, between the cans of coffee and jars of jam, whispers of the woods dust the just-picked crops and graze the gossipers, while the locals share brief knowing glances through the charged air.

"I'm telling you," a girl squeals into her phone. She's young, maybe fourteen, with blonde hair carefully styled in two buns on her head, just above a delicately folded, designer bandana. Her fashionable wool-lined hiking boots and freshly applied lip-gloss expose her as a tourist. She trails behind her younger brother and parents, who fawn over apple-butter and canned beans. The entire family wears matching I heart Cherokee National Forest T-shirts. "Seriously, if my parents and crazy brother would ever shut up, they would've heard her. All along the creek. Singing. I couldn't make out the words, but her voice was real high, and now the tune's stuck in my head."

She picks up a jar of chow-chow, turning it curiously in her free hand before returning it to the table. "No, it was definitely a she. And it was more of a lulling, slow song. I'm sure I'll catch myself humming it next time I paint my nails. I don't think I'll ever be able to forget it." The girl drifts through the door and into a rocker out front.

"Was that your daughter?" A college student asks her parents, but before they can reply, he continues. "You hiked Sally's Hole?...Because," —he leans over the tomatoes— "I camped there one night."

"No way!" The brother pushes between his parents to listen.

"Yeah, my friends and I camped out there once. I mean, the trees are real tall with crazy shadows, and the creek gives off this faint, high-pitched sound with the current. Of course, we were going to camp out there. I mean, the bear sign is real faded, so who knows when there were actually bears."

"Yeah." The brother smiles as if he knows.

"And the ghosts? Well, you know how those stories are. My

girlfriend's from around here, so she tried to warn us, but come on, ghosts? Besides, if there's a ghost out there, all the more reason to go, right? Or at least that's what I thought until I saw her."

"You *saw* her?" The boy's now entranced.

"Oh, yeah. We were sitting at our campfire next to the creek. Our tents were up, and we'd just opened the first beers of the night. I turned to grab a lighter for my friend, and there she was, standing between those tall trees. Quiet. Still. She was looking right at me. She was young. Real young and pretty. Maybe eighteen. And she was holding something small close to her chest. That's when I made the mistake of blinking. After that, there was nothing but the music of the creek. My girlfriend was right."

"Whoa." The boy stumbles back.

The father scowls at the student before placing his arm around the boy's shoulder. "Come on, son."

"I stayed out there once too." A voice rises from a stack of hay bales behind the student. "One night, when I first moved out here, before I knew better. One night was enough."

The student walks over to sit facing the man. The hay pricks through his denim and punctures his flesh, leaving tiny irritations that'll bother him for days. "Go on."

The man snuffs his spent cigarette and continues, his words heavy with tar and smoke, his voice stained and weak from the nicotine. "It was pitch black, and all I could hear was the water and the frogs and the cicadas. I let it lull me right to sleep, and I slept good until the crying woke me. Crying, loud and shrill. I stepped out of my tent, but there was nothing except crying., It didn't last all night."

"No?" The student's now as rapt as the boy had been.

"It was worse. It faded away, but once I started to doze off, the crying returned. It came and went all night. Loud and shrill, and then fade away, just to return a while later. The next morning, I drove around the entire site. I was certain there must've been a mother walking her colicky baby the whole night through, and I was going to find her. Maybe she needed help. Maybe she could help me. But there wasn't a sign of anyone else having camped. No tents. No burnt wood. No cigarette butts. Nothing but that cry lingering with me. I still hear it, you know. It haunts me some nights." His fresh cigarette shakes in his hand as he tries to light it.

"I didn't see anything." At some point the teen has left her rocker to be drawn into the conversation. "I only heard the singing. But my brother says he saw something, for what it's worth."

"I *did* see something." The brother has abandoned their parents at the cashier. "You know how it was *super* foggy?"

"Yeah, so?" says his sister.

The boy turns from his disbelieving sibling to address the captive audience on the hay bales. "Yeah, well, we were hiking by the creek, and it was foggy. We walked by the Hole, and... I saw him when I looked up. Him *and* his cabin at the top of the ridge over the Hole. He was just standing there right in front of their cabin, and he was staring down at us."

"You saw Old Joe himself," says the man with the cigarette. "There's not many who can claim that."

His sister shifts her weight. "What did you do?"

"I ran to catch up with you guys," says the boy. "What'd you think I'd do, invite him to join us?"

"All right, you two. Let's go," their mother calls from the door.

"Like you even know what Old Joe looks like," the sister continues as they turn to follow their parents.

"I do now. I just told you I saw him."

"What you saw was an internet article on ghosts." She knocks his shoulder.

"I read about the hiking trail, that's all."

The door shuts behind them, and I glance at my wife behind the worn cash register. She nods knowingly before turning to straighten the canned beets.

Sightings at Sally's Hole have been a part of life here for nearing a century. The France farm overlooked the water hole and the river, which was just as full of life and prime for fishing then as it is now. Legend has it, at the end of a hard day's work, with rolled tobacco between his chapped lips, Old Joe liked to stand at the edge of his farmland, on the top of the ravine, and look down at the currents to watch life, and maybe dinner, swim by. Joe and Sally France were a well-respected, prominent couple... until the day they weren't.

I've seen that moment relived, at dusk when the fog comes in and the shadows shift. Sally's holding that poor boy to her breast, soothing his cries with kisses and a lullaby, tears streaming down her cheeks all the while. Step by step, she walks into the water of what's now called Sally's Hole, the boy crying, Sally singing until they both fade into the tepid pool.

And Old Joe? Why, he does like he always does; he stands and watches.

For want of water.

Survival

By Brenda G'Fellers

Genre: Horror

Keywords: rabies, July 4th, dogs, Kentucky, family, sisters, poverty

CW: parental abuse, dog attack

Summer 1963 was truly another time and place. John F. Kennedy was President, and the War on Poverty was a dream he promoted. I was thirteen and had just finished eighth grade. I lived in the midst of the poverty Kennedy wanted to fight, in Letcher County, Kentucky. My family resided about ten miles outside of Whitesburg, the county seat, in the small community of Colson. There was no free lunch program at school, no SNAP, and free government commodities such as meat, cheese, rice, and peanut butter were only available from time to time. We didn't have indoor plumbing; all our water came from a fresh-water spring about a quarter mile down the holler.

There was minimal electricity in the little house and its five rooms, so each room had a single overhead light, a bare bulb hanging in the center. There was wiring for an electric range, and I learned how to dry socks and underwear in that oven without letting them catch fire. We had no money for the doctor or for coal to heat the ramshackle house. We lived, quite literally, on the wrong side of the tracks and would walk them with buckets in hand to glean fallen coal we could use for heating.

My family? At that point, there were six of us children plus my mother and father. My father, dark-haired and handsome, resembled a young Andy Griffith, and standing tall at 6'4", he was a mere twenty years older than me. He was an auto mechanic by trade and an alcoholic by genes and choice. My mother, petite and brown-haired but so pretty, was as care worn as she was clever and determined to take advantage of any break that might come along. I was the eldest child, followed by Trish, age eleven, and Jackie, age nine. Bill, the only boy, was five, Pamma was three, and Yvonne, the baby, was just a few months old. Most of us were blond, but as the eldest, my hair had darkened to brown.

We all showed the slimness that comes from never needing to be told to clean our plates.

Our little house, like so many in Letcher County, was sandwiched between mountains in a narrow valley. On our side of the tracks, there was also another little house with a worn gray plank exterior that contrasted our home's brown siding. A large family lived there, too, the Longs. The patriarch, sons, daughters, and sons-in-law were long and tall, rangy even. The mother, Mrs. Long, was short and round.

Families sometimes have beliefs that seem strange to outsiders, and the Longs believed that girls who went to high school automatically became pregnant. When their beautiful younger daughter, Lucy, completed eighth grade, the family kept her at home the following school year. When officials came knocking, a compromise was reached. Lucy repeated her eighth grade year and turned sixteen the following summer, at which time she dropped out.

It was a gorgeous, hot July fourth. The sky was bright blue with but a few scattered white clouds. Our father had gone to the garage to work and had promised to pick up some fireworks afterward. He promised to return before dark, so we waited anxiously at home.

The Long family stood in their clean-swept yard, observing a family fourth of July tradition. After their fried chicken, green bean, and cornbread dinner, the family celebrated with special treats. Each family member, from Mr. Long all the way to his beautiful blond, brown-eyed granddaughter, received their own half-gallon of ice cream and a watermelon. My siblings and I watched hungrily from across the dirt road that separated the two small houses.

A breeze began to blow, carrying a strange sound to us from the woods that grew up the mountain. A low, rumbling growl, increasing to a howl, moving nearer then returning to a rumbling growl. Suddenly chilled despite the heat, we turned to look, as did the Longs.

A red, mangy dog with foam around its mouth had made that horrific sound. Mr. Long yelled for his family to get indoors, but that dog moved faster than anyone could. It ran from the woods, straight across the bare yard, and leapt at Mrs. Long, tearing at her arm. She screamed as blood poured from her left elbow.

The dog kept running, continuing on its path once it'd finished with Mrs. Long, reaching the railroad tracks where it ran in the opposite direction of Whitesburg.

Things happened quickly after that. The older daughter, Bonnie, ran into the house to get towels to wrap her mother's arm while the three sons and Mr. Long grabbed their rifles. The son-in-law started the car, tucked Mrs. Long, Lucy, Bonnie, and his little daughter into the back seat, and headed for the hospital while the father and sons set off down the tracks, moving at a lope as they followed the dog.

My sisters and I sat numbly across the drive, overcome by fear brought on by the chaos then sudden silence. It was too hot to stay inside despite any threat, so we waited, uncertain what to do next.

One of my sisters said she was thirsty, but none of us moved because we all knew the water bucket was low, and we were all tired by the time one of the Long boys loped back down the tracks into their yard. "What's going on?" I yelled. "Did you get it?"

"Not yet." He climbed into the family's aged pickup truck. "We will, though. It's got to be tested. It has to be mad." And then he was gone, driving off to meet his father and brothers.

The afternoon continued to pass, and we brought blankets out to lie on in the shade, hoping to escape the worst of the heat, but we continued to keep wary eyes and ears on the forest. "Girls," our mother called. "Keep an eye on the young ones and use water sparingly." We were thirsty. Who wouldn't be? But thinking about it made it worse, and our mother wouldn't send us for water because it was far too dangerous.

We carried the blankets back inside when the sun began setting, and each of us took a carefully measured drink of water. Now, only about an inch remained in the bucket. "Just wait," said Mama. "Your dad will be here. Either he'll go to the spring by himself, or he'll go with you. Either way, it'll be all right."

Dusk came, but no one had returned to the Longs' house, and there was no relief from the heat until lights crossed the tracks; our father was home at last. We ran for the car to tell him what had happened, but he rapidly dismissed us. "Get into the house. I'm hungry and thirsty."

None of us bothered to ask about the fireworks because we knew too well how he often broke the best of promises.

When Mama explained about the small amount of water in the bucket, his reaction was unpleasant but, in hindsight, typical. "I worked all day in the heat so this bunch of scared little girls can go together up to the spring. But I tell you what. I'll turn the car around and shine the headlights up the holler to help them see." Those lights wouldn't shine far into the trees, but there was no use in our protesting; we had all felt the back of his hand or his belt more than once.

Trish and I decided we'd go together since we were the eldest, but we were so afraid we trembled. Jackie wanted to go too, but I told her no. "It's dark, and the path is barely wide enough for two."

Hand in hand, each with a bucket, Trish and I left the house, crossed the yard, and headed up the path to the spring.

We heard night sounds as we walked, but we reached the water without incident. Trish stooped and filled her bucket while I stood lookout, then it was my turn. I bent to fill mine, looking up in horror when I heard a growl behind me. Terrified, I dropped my bucket and reached blindly behind me, grabbing something by the neck I was intent on choking.

"Brenda!" Trish screamed. "Let go! It's Jackie. It's only Jackie!"

I let go, and Jackie fell to the ground, coughing, rubbing her neck, crying, her voice raspy. "I'm sorry. I just wanted to come with you. I didn't mean to scare you."

I still shook as I filled the second bucket and the three of us walked home. There was no dog and no dog attack, just a younger sister's foolish prank and the potential of our father's wrath.

We carried our buckets into the house and through to the kitchen as we shared our tale with the family. Our father had the water he wanted. Jackie had suffered no physical harm and was told she got what she deserved for scaring people on such a dark and frightening night.

The following day, we learned the Longs had caught and killed the dog. Tests showed it was rabid, so Mrs. Long had to endure a long series of required shots. Jackie continued playing occasional tricks but never another like she had. Six months later, we moved back to Tennessee, and our lives gradually began to improve.

We still sometimes talk of that night, about the terror we'd faced as children. Trish says she can still hear my scream, filled with both rage and fear. And still, when I'm alone, I wonder what fear might lead us to do, and I know that night is when I labeled myself both a fighter and a survivor.

A gift or a curse? You decide.

Born With a Veil

By Jules Corriere

Genre: Paranormal

Keywords: family, ghosts, Georgia, the sight

I was born with a veil on my face. That's what my grandmother called it. She's the one who saw it first, when she helped bring me into the world. A medicine woman of sorts, my grandmother nursed and midwifed throughout the foothills of Franklin County. From the time I was old enough to walk, I accompanied her on these visits. She raised me, teaching me about the different root cures that were passed on to her, cures that she passed on to my mother, who didn't have faith in the old ways and died in the hospital of a far-away town. I remember the lights, bright and white, in the sterile place where the only living things inside were the dying people. I remember the colorless hallways and the white-capped nurses, silently gliding through wings that were barren of anything I found familiar. No flowers were allowed on the ward, nothing as a reminder of home or happiness... or hope. The space seems so blank and long ago, I sometimes have trouble remembering my mother's last days there. Or remembering my mother at all, the way her eyes used to smile when she talked to me. Even today, I can only see her when I close my eyes and think of her back at the cabin we shared with my grandparents.

I caught myself trying to see her as I walked the long trail home after one of my grandmother's healing visits. I almost knew this path by heart, so I felt confident closing my eyes while I skipped alongside her. Our pace was quicker than usual, as Gumlog was more than a comfortable day's walk, and Grandma always liked to get home before dark. We often rode together on our Tennessee Walker when the visits were this far away, but my grandfather had taken Goldie into the hills a few days before on his annual trip to collect ginseng. He still wasn't back when Grandma got the call to tend Mrs. Wellborne.

It was on this walk, along the winding wooded trail, that my grandmother told me about the veil. In hindsight, this revelation wasn't planned, but it had become warranted.

I was skipping along, squeezing my eyes tight, trying to see my mother, but I stopped when I felt a hazy breeze. There was a sweet smell in the air, riding over the familiar scent of damp earth and wood rot. Violets, maybe, but too delicate to tell, a fragrance so fragile that if I breathed in too hard, it might shatter. I opened my eyes and looked around, only to see a lady, a real fancy dresser all in white. My mother was a fancy dresser too, so I thought it was her walking down the road.

"Mama? Mama! Over here!" I flew after her, but the woman kept going.

"Fanny!" Grandma called sharply. "Get back here!"

I continued running, panting, almost screaming. "I'm going to meet Mama!"

"No, Fanny! Come here now!"

My grandmother's voice jolted me, and my head jerked back as I came to a full stop. Red Georgia clay kicked up around my ankles. Suddenly, the fancy dresser turned and disappeared into the woods, evaporating into the shadows and leaving me alone. I turned back and walked toward my Grandmother, retracing my footsteps.

When I reached Grandma, she spun forward and continued the journey without saying a word. We walked maybe another mile then she pulled me onto a log.

"Let's rest our feet here."

We sat under the trees, a canopy of sycamores and tulip poplars, still alive in vibrant crimsons and yellows. Brown thrashers and wrens called to each other as they organized their long flight south. It was late in the season for these birds; they'd soon be flying using only their instincts to guide their way. Grandma and I remained silent under their chatter. I imagined them having a conversation, reminding each other of directions and the best places to stop along the way, just as Grandma and I had done before we set out for Gumlog. A tiny sweat bee landed on my knee, and I watched it walk across the scar from when I crawled too close to the woodstove. I don't remember what happened, but I'd be forever reminded by the patchy discoloration the accident left behind.

Grandma looked at me, not hard, as she often did when I was in trouble, but delicate, almost watery, gentle enough I could ask her a question.

"Why wouldn't you let me go to her?"

"She wasn't who you thought she was. And this isn't the right time of day to be walking with spirits."

"You mean she wasn't real?"

"Oh, she was very real. As real as you and me. She once walked and talked on this earth, like we're doing right now. But she's on the other side of the veil. Most times, spirits just want to be remembered. They show themselves and that's that. Sometimes, they need to pass on some news to people on this side. But every once in a while, there's one that wants something more. That lady probably just wanted to be remembered. But I don't want you walking with a spirit when the time's not right. That's why I called you back."

I thought about this and then asked Grandma, "How did she know I'd see her?"

Grandma looked back to the trail, her eyes focused on something I couldn't see, and her words were as soft as smoke. "You were born with a veil on your face. I was too, but you were born with a half veil. That means you can see things, people and ideas that used to be, but I was born with a full veil. That means I see toward the future."

In that moment, pictures flashed in my mind, and ideas I'd wondered over began making sense. A flood of moments and questions stood out, memories I had but weren't mine, all assembling in a giant collage I could see just behind my eyes. My confusion snapped into hard focus as I tried putting it together. "So that's how you know if someone you're helping will get well or die, like you said Mrs. Wellborne probably won't make it." I waited for her to agree and felt myself reach toward understanding, but Grandma's words pulled my spirit back to hold me in line.

"The veil is a gift best kept to yourself. It's a quiet gift. For your own good, it's better not to let anyone else know. Most of those who find out will try to use it, and those who don't understand will be afraid."

"I'm afraid too." I felt powerful, knowing I shared a gift with my Grandmother, but at the same time I was like those people she spoke of. I was afraid of what I didn't understand.

"Aren't you scared of knowing someone is going to die?" I looked down at my scar as I traced the outline.

"Oh, no, sweetheart. Only God knows those things. What I see is more like patterns and pictures. Take that scar you're tracing. What do you see?"

"I don't know. It's lighter than the rest of my skin."

"Look beyond that. Look into it. What comes to mind?"

"Well, the scar isn't shaped like this, but when I look at it, it sort of makes me think of a bee hive."

Grandma smiled softly. "Do you remember when that happened to you?"

"No, I was just a baby."

"It was a bad burn. We cleaned it and then covered it with honey. Every day we covered it with honey to keep it from flaming up until it healed. The bee hive is a picture from your past. Pictures and patterns. You do have the gift. And you shouldn't be afraid of it."

I gazed at her, my thoughts a fog of questions.

"I know things by looking at pictures and patterns too," Grandma continued. "I try to make sense of them when I'm helping folks. Sometimes, the pictures show me what to do. Other times, they show me what might happen. Take Mrs. Wellborne. Yes, I did tell you that I didn't think we'd be making another trip back to help her. What I meant is this— if the pattern stays the same, if the weather stays damp and cool, and the cracks in her floor aren't covered, then her cough will settle in. She'll be too cold to get up and move it out of her lungs, and pneumonia's gonna take her. Now, if that pattern changes, she's got a chance. But when we tended her, I saw her, in my mind, wearing a wedding dress. There's only two occasions a woman wears that dress, when she gets married and when she gets buried. And Mrs. Wellborne is already married."

I pondered this before I asked, "Will I see the future, too?"

"No. The half veil sees the present and the past. Remember?"

"Too bad. I wish I could see the future."

Just then, the calling birds flew out of the trees in tandem, all of them knowing exactly the direction the others were taking, an impeccable synchrony, while a perfectly-timed blood-red maple leaf lofted down to land between us on the log.

Grandma tapped me on the nose with it then hugged me. It was my signal she was done talking. I was ready for the last leg of our journey, and a silent, burning excitement filled me along the way. I clearly remember this day as the moment I discovered a new way of seeing the world. I now knew how to read the things I saw with open eyes and understood that some things are better seen with them closed.

I practiced both on that long road home.

We'd walk that road together many times over the years to come. We walked it for Mrs. Wellborne's funeral. We walked it after Grandma delivered a set of twins, and I got to help. I walked it with her as an adult, on a day like the day I learned of my gift, without fear even though I knew it wasn't the right time to be walking with spirits. Grandma, dressed in her fanciest white dress, walked beside me as I carried a basket of violets to place on her gravestone.

Don't pick the flowers.

The Neighbors
are Fantastic

By Jeanne G'Fellers

Genre: Paranormal

Keywords: spirits, wildlife, Tennessee, family

The white house with black shutters on Woods Drive felt like home the moment we pulled into the sloping drive. The home had been built in 1949 then renovated in 2010 to include a third bedroom and a second bath, but the house still held much of its original charm. It looked like a quaint fairytale cottage, and I'd wanted to live there from the first moment I'd seen the online rental listing. It was just my wife, Anna, myself, and our two teenage sons, a quiet little family of four, so this home would be perfect. We had three cats as well, and the homeowner had already said they were welcome. Best of all was the gorgeous sunroom at the back of the house just off the master bedroom.

The cats were going to love that feature.

I wanted the home even more when we stepped out the back door and onto the covered porch. It was peaceful there. The house was situated between Johnson City and Elizabethton and was near a local college and university, off a busier road but tucked back enough that we couldn't hear the traffic. It was the perfect location, and the neighboring lot had never been cleared or built upon, so it was thick with trees. But behind and beside the house... My heart soared when I saw the raised garden beds. This home, with its well-established garden, was exactly what we'd been searching for.

"What do you think, honey?" I grinned hopefully at Anna, and she nodded.

"It's got character, the neighborhood is quiet, and I adore the back deck." She leaned in to speak in my ear. "And you've done nothing but talk about this place since you found the ad. Let's go for it."

The boys loved their spaces, so we signed the lease and paid our deposit the very next day then moved from our current rental within the month. It was already September, so there wasn't much to do but maintain the yard and keep the garden beds clean until next year, which we happily did, but our little white house soon proved unique in ways we hadn't expected. First, there was the wildlife, which wasn't your run-of-the-mill racoon in the trash cans. Racoons were around, of course, and the squirrels repeatedly proved they could conquer the best made squirrel-proof bird feeder, but there was something deep and incredible going on where the wildlife was concerned.

There were all manner of birds, including several species not commonly seen in Northeast Tennessee, so we invested in a book to identify them. And there was the neighborhood overfed cat who visited us each day. No one seemed to claim him, so we named him Clyde for lack of his real name. He would lay in the driveway, orange and fabulously fluffy as he bathed, and he sometimes sprawled across the road in front of the house to sun himself. A possum nonchalantly hung out on our back porch whether we were sitting there or not, and a family of racoons, mama and her four kits, nibbled on Clyde's cat food every evening while we sat watching. This place was rife with polite animals and gorgeous flowers, but even when it grew cold outside and the flowers faded, the animals and the majority of the birds remained, even Clyde, who slept on a blanket we placed on the porch swing.

And our inside cats? Yes, they loved the sunroom and often watched the birds and squirrels, but they watched the woods in the empty lot even more, peering into the trees for hours on end. We weren't sure what they were staring at, but they took turns being rapt by it.

Late that fall, Anna texted pictures of the house and property to a friend in West Virginia, and her response was swift. "Tanya wants to know if the house is haunted."

"Why did she say that?" I asked.

"Because of this." Anna held up her phone so I could see the pictures she'd taken. Every image had a strange mist across it.

"She says it's spirit smoke."

"No." I gave her back the phone. "If anyone here knows about such things it's me, and this house isn't haunted." But the wooded lot next door was a different matter. I'd already pondered this at some length. I'm an eclectic witch, sometimes called a green witch. I've experienced natural magic on many occasions, and I knew the wooded lot had something residing in it, a presence, an entity I couldn't easily define. I'm certain that's why no one had built there, but our house and gardens weren't haunted. Still, I began looking for evidence to prove my suspicions, even though I was confident we were safe within our home. I'd saged the house, placed charged crystals in the corners, and hung wards over all the doors when we'd moved in. In hindsight, however, my protections might have actually cleared a path because whatever resided in those woods knew I was aware of their presence.

By the new year, it wanted to say hello, and our doorbell, which it chose to speak through, was *outside* the house.

"Is someone at the door?" Anna called from our bedroom. The doorbell, an older electronic model, had remote chimes that were located in our bedroom at the back of the house. You could set the bells to play different tunes including "Happy Birthday" and "We Wish You a Merry Christmas," but we'd set it to a traditional ding-dong when we'd moved in.

"I dunno. Did the doorbell ring?" I was in the kitchen tending the sourdough we'd nursed through the winter. "Oh, I hear it. Hold on." I dried my hands and headed toward the door, only to find no one was there.

"Who is it?" Anna now stood behind me.

"Some kid playing a prank, I guess." I shrugged and closed the door, trying to ignore my prickling arm hair.

"There aren't any kids in this neighborhood that I've seen." Anna scratched her head. "Maybe someone's—"

The doorbell began playing "Auld Lang Syne," and this

time I was close enough to fling open the door before the music ended. But again, no one was there. "That's weird." I shut and locked the door then leaned against it, looking at Anna who stared past me to the three glass panes in the door's top portion.

"Yeah, weird." We both shook off the incident and returned to what we were doing, but the doorbell rang again for no reason twice the next day, each time a different song, and again a few days after that.

"The doorbell is messed up," said our elder son the second time he'd answered the door to find an empty porch one afternoon. "You want me to fix it?"

"No, I'll look myself if it doesn't quit." That evening the doorbell rang fourteen times, each time with a different tune, and I told everyone not to open the door lest we let something inside we didn't want. Whatever our magical neighbor was selling, we weren't buying, especially when it was dark outside.

The next day, I climbed onto a step stool and opened the doorbell's remote housing to examine the wiring. "You're kidding me." I'm certain I was pale, but I managed to call for Anna so she could look for herself and stepped off the stool so she could take my place.

"The wires are disconnected." She put the cover back on the chimes, screwed it down, and headed to the front door with the screwdriver in hand. "We'll get to the bottom of..." The other side of the doorbell was disconnected too.

"It shouldn't be working at all." But it obviously was, even when actual people came to visit.

"I don't know what the—" She startled when the doorbell rang with us standing outside, playing "We Three Kings" for an otherwise empty house.

"Well now." I stepped from the porch to stare at the wooded lot. "I think Tanya was right about spirit smoke. Something is afoot, but I don't think it's in the house."

"Yet." Anna screwed the cover back on the doorbell and

opened the screen door, pausing long enough to look over her shoulder at me. "This is your territory, so fix it."

The doorbell quit ringing as often after that, and I prayed the problem had solved itself or at least become tolerable. The entity in the woods had made its presence known then retreated. Fair enough. We could live with that and did so happily until later that spring when Anna called me to the back porch late one sunny afternoon.

"Come here." She patted the space beside her on the porch swing then pointed to the wooded lot. "Look. Do you see what I do?"

I squinted into the sunlight above the trees. "What are they? Swarming insects?"

"I thought so at first, but they're too big."

"Birds?" I squinted harder. "No, birds don't move like that." These were too big to be either hummingbirds or insects, but they were winged nonetheless. "What are they?"

"Fairies." My Catholic-raised spouse had just claimed we were seeing fairies. Now I knew beyond a doubt that those woods were occupied by something greater than either of us.

The next full moon, the crystals I set out to charge were so energy-filled that they pulsed not only in my hand but all the way up my arm and into my shoulder. "Magical indeed." I placed those in our home's corners, renewed the household wards, and went back to business as usual, especially the gardens, which were in need of attention now that the flowers were in bloom.

The doorbell problem returned the next week, and the animals brought their friends, but now they were sitting curled beneath the porch swing; possums and racoons were napping side-by-side under our feet while Clyde slept on the back porch rug. The furry menagerie was sweet and wonderful if not a bit Disney's Snow White-ish, but the doorbell problem? It was time I had a chat with our invisible neighbor, so the next morning I sat alone on the back porch steps, facing the woods, my hands folded in my lap as I peered into the trees.

"Hi, there. Look, I know you're there. I really do. We *all* know you're there. And we respect that those woods are your space, but can you please lay off the doorbell? Thanks." I received no direct reply, but the doorbell stopped ringing even when there was a flesh-and-blood person pressing the button.

Success. This witch can get things done when she puts her mind to it, but I admit I let that success go to my head, allowing things to slide afterward, mostly forgetting about the potential problem next door until June.

I was working along the edge of the driveway against the wooded lot, pulling weeds from around the Bleeding Hearts, when I saw one of the irises had broken near its base. It wouldn't survive the day on the driveway pavement, so I broke if off, holding it up to admire the watercolor-like purples and blues. This garden was rich, and I appreciated everything it gave us, but we only had large vases in the house, so one flower became two became...

"Don't. Stop. Please!" The voice was childlike.

"Who said that?" My skin prickled as I stood up to look around, shivering when I realized the voice had come from the woods. But there was no one down there. The lot had a steep incline, and the ground beneath the trees was covered in poison ivy, Virginia creeper, and undergrowth until it was impossible to walk across. It was suddenly no longer a matter of recognizing the entity next door or asking it to quit playing with the doorbell. The situation had progressed until it was *speaking* to me.

"Don't pick the flowers." This time the voice, while still childlike, was insistent.

"Okay. Sorry." I backed from the driveway and all the way into the house, staring into the woods as I went. It wasn't that I didn't believe in the entity. I knew full well it was there. It represented life and energy and all things wonderful, but...

"Here." I shoved two irises at Anna and collapsed into my recliner beside her.

"Um, thanks." She looked from the flowers to me, furrowing her brows. "What's wrong?"

"It spoke to me." My voice and everything about me shook from the experience.

"Who spoke to you?"

"The, the entity in the woods. It told me not to pick the flowers."

"Really?" She held the irises at arms' length. "Let me get some water for these."

"Yeah." I returned to my thoughts, pondering how the house and property was no longer just a rental. It'd become a lesson in respect and boundaries. If the entity could respect that our home was off limits and quit ringing the doorbell, the least I could do was not pick the flowers along its borders.

Late that summer, we moved from the house on Woods Drive because I'd found a teaching job in another state. I loathed leaving our fairytale cottage behind, but paying the rent and feeding my family outweighed the magic in the woods. Living there, however, has had a lingering effect on me. The message was clear, and I learned the lesson well. Magical boundaries are there for good reason. To that end, I no longer buy flowers unless they're to plant, and I will not, under any circumstances, pick flowers, even those in my own yard, because they might actually belong to someone or something else.

Specifics make or break wishes... and families

Pieces and Parts

By Anne G'Fellers-Mason

Genre: Horror

Keywords: magic, family, siblings

CW: cancer, mild gore

Aboy in a pirate costume sat alone at the end of the bleachers. No one approached him or came by to check on him. For a moment in time, he was completely alone, and he relished it. It was the perfect kind of solitude, the kind that can only be achieved in a crowded room. The party and everyone involved were gathered at the other end of the gymnasium, clustered under the basketball goal. They moved from one lopsided booth to another, sampling the wares, playing the games, having their fortunes told, and other "festive" things. Laughter and merriment hung in the air, along with the occasional gasp or other forced emotion, but the young pirate wanted none of it. All he wanted was some space to himself and his book.

He paused to adjust the stupid, clingy tunic that kept riding up, and turned the page. He was halfway through Mary Shelley's *Frankenstein*, so he took a moment to silently celebrate his accomplishment. A slight smile played across his lips, and he had no desire at all to look for his family. They were down there somewhere, raising money for Devin. They were always raising money for Devin. In fact, his family had been the primary beneficiaries of the Fall Festival for the past five years. Multiple surgeries and medical treatments are expensive, and doubly so when it's two children you have going under the knife. Of course, only Devin benefited from it all. Tucker was always the loser, loser of blood, of bone marrow, of a kidney. He was born solely to keep his brother alive, a donor baby.

Tucker paused only long enough to peer out the gym's open doors, suffering the mountains a look as more shouts of joy rose from the gym floor. Crowds of smiling faces had never been his thing, but smiling faces were what greeted him every time in the hospital when everything hurt. The air then was too heavy, and all he wanted to do was sleep, but he couldn't because of those stupid smiling faces. They'd peer down at him and shake him to say, "Devin's doing so well. Aren't you glad to hear it?" Tucker didn't feel glad those days, but he felt glad now. He was glad anytime he was left alone with a good book in his hands. Books were really all he had. He couldn't ride bikes or play sports or chase lightning bugs on a summer night. He couldn't do anything that might risk energy to his person because Devin might need that part someday. Tucker was not a real boy of ten. Rather, like Frankenstein's Monster, he was pieces and parts.

The damn tunic rolled up again, so Tucker straightened it with a little more force, adding a disgruntled huff.

"Good book?"

Tucker startled at the voice and looked up to see a tall, gaunt man standing before him. He hadn't seen or heard the man approach, but maybe that wasn't much of a surprise; after all, the man looked like he could blow away with a good puff, so how much noise could he possibly make?

"Good book?" The man asked again, something akin to a smile spreading across his thin face. If it weren't for the twinkle in his eye, Tucker would've sworn he was ill. Tucker had spent most of his life in hospitals, so he knew sickness when he saw it, but this man was difficult to place.

"Yeah," Tucker replied, suddenly aware the man had asked him the same question twice.

"*Frankenstein*, tough read for a boy your age." The man placed one bony knee on the bleachers and leaned in, his lean fingers entwining like branches on top of his thigh.

"I get it," Tucker responded with confidence.

"I bet you do." The man tilted his head. "Who's your favorite character? No, wait, let me guess." The man took one, pale finger and placed it over his colorless lips, pondering for a moment. "Dr. Frankenstein?"

"Nope." Tucker shook his head. "The Monster."

"Really?" The twinkle in the man's eyes grew to a gleam.

"Yeah, he didn't choose his life. It was forced upon him."

"And what about you?" the man inquired, leaning closer. "Was your life forced upon you?"

Tucker's tongue stuck in the back of his throat and he faltered. This was too much on point. The man seemed to sense his discomfort and eased back, giving Tucker breathing space.

"That your family?" The man asked, his eyes flickering to the booth with the shoddily drawn pirate ship stuck to it.

"Yeah," Tucker lamented.

"Pirates, huh?"

Tucker sighed. "My Mom's idea."

"And the boy with the oxygen tank is...?"

"My brother, Devin. He's got leukemia."

The man clicked his tongue with exaggerated concern. "How awful. But your parents must be pleased that you're healthy and strong."

This was so wrong Tucker almost laughed. "They don't care about me." The words rolled out of his mouth before he could stop them.

"Oh, now surely that's not true." The man leaned in for a third time, and Tucker found himself looking directly into the man's sunken eyes. They were a curious, swirling mix of colors, and Tucker sensed himself cracking open like an egg. Feelings and emotions he'd kept to himself came spilling out. At first he was afraid, terrified even, but then fear gave way to anger, anger at his parents, at his brother, at any higher power that existed or had ever existed.

"No, they don't care. They only had me to fix him. They didn't want me, not really. They wanted Devin. All they need me for is parts, parts for him, so he won't die. I can't go to school, 'cause I might get sick. I can't ride a bike, or a horse, or go camping 'cause I might break something. I don't have any friends. I've never been out of the state. I've never done anything, and I'm ten years old, and they don't even care. They took my kidney, and it hurt a lot. Then when I woke up crying in the hospital because it hurt so bad, do you know what my parents told me?"

The man shook his head, but his eyes stayed fixed on Tucker's, urging him on.

"They said..." Tucker took a deep breath. "'Hush now. You have to be strong for Devin.'"

Everything that could be spilled was now on the floor, and Tucker felt lightheaded, like it'd been blood instead of resentments he'd been spilling. He set down his book and pulled his arms around his knees to fight off the sudden chill. The carnival noises were distant and fuzzy, but the man was clear.

"Who are you?" Tucker asked, but his voice sounded distorted to his own ears.

"A friend," the man replied in a warmer tone. "And a purveyor of magic." He reached out with one hand to pull a large coin from behind Tucker's ear.

This was recognizable, so Tucker dropped his arms, now more at ease. "That's not magic. It was hidden up your sleeve."

"Perhaps it was," the man replied. He released the coin, but it didn't fall to the ground. Rather, it floated in the air as Tucker gasped. There were no wires when he felt for them and... The coin began to rotate, and Tucker could not take his eyes off the spinning silver.

"What do you fear?" the man asked. "Death?"

Tucker shook his head. "We're all gonna die."

"Then what do *you* fear?"

"Not living." Tucker spoke in a small voice.

"And what do you want more than anything in this world?"

"To be whole again."

The man snatched the coin from the air, and Tucker startled back to reality. The man smiled when he looked up, but it wasn't warm this time; it was something else entirely.

"Tucker! We're taking a family picture!" His mother's voice

cut through the haze, and Tucker turned his head quickly to the left, but when he looked back, the man was gone.

· · · · · · · · · · ● ● ● ● ● ● ● ● ● ● ● ● · · · · · · · · · · ·

That night, Tucker read under his blanket with his flashlight, like usual, but the strange man kept running through his mind. He'd looked for him the rest of the evening, but it'd been to no avail, and he was still pondering this fact as he drifted to sleep, the sound of his brother's breathing machine heavy and loud in the next room.

When Tucker woke the next morning, he instantly knew something was different. He felt odd but good, really, really good, like he could scale a mountain or run to the moon and back. He couldn't remember the last time he'd felt this good or so optimistic.

He bounded out of bed as something fell from his covers, landing at his feet. Tucker picked it up and turned it over. It was a note, and written across the yellowed paper in thick, dark letters were the words, "Your wish has been granted."

"Who knows." He shoved the note into his pajama pants and left his room with purposed steps. Today, he was going outside, and he was going to stay there until the sun slipped from the sky no matter what his mother said. But before he reached his parents' room, Tucker entered his brother's. He needed to share his good fortune, to gloat.

"Devin!" Tucker whooped, but his voice died in his throat.

The room was quiet, far too quiet. The breathing machine was turned off and the sheets were... Tucker gulped. The sheets were splashed with red.

He approached the bed even though he didn't want to. With a shaking hand, he threw back the crimson covers, choking back a scream as he looked. There were gaping holes all over Devin's body. Someone had come, taken what they wanted, and left the rest to rot.

Tucker closed his eyes, but the image of his brother's body was forever burned in his mind. His wish, though indirect, had been granted, but it'd lacked critical specifics.

Firsthand experience is often the best teacher.

As Light Fades

By Kristin Pearson

Genre: Paranormal

Keywords: genealogy, coal country, Kentucky, cemetery, family

CW: poverty, death

Maggie flipped off the microfilm reader's light and rubbed her eyes. She'd had enough of the *Hazard Herald*, at least for now. The articles were starting to blur together, never a good sign when she was hunting for yet another obituary.

The branches of her family tree were filling out quite nicely. The Germans, Irish, and even Quakers on her mother's side had left records galore. But now that Maggie was digging through her father's convoluted family history in the hills and hollers of Eastern Kentucky, she had a feeling that skeletons were waiting to be uncovered, whether they wanted it or not.

Maggie had collected quite a few interesting facts in the small town that had once been entirely dependent on coal. The mining companies had mostly closed and moved on, and many of the people had moved on too, up to Cincinnati, Louisville, Dayton, and other manufacturing towns. But some people, once rooted, had never left.

A gentle chime sounded, and a voice came over the loudspeaker: "The Perry County Public Library will be closing in fifteen minutes." Maggie gathered her printouts, put her microfilm reel in the return box, and exited the genealogy department. Waving a farewell to the sole reference staff on duty, she walked to the exit and squinted into the summer evening sun. Daylight would last at least another hour, so Maggie decided to swing by the old coal camp cemetery before heading home through the Cumberland Gap.

· ·

Maggie's Prius hummed as she guided it around the bends of the narrow county road. She always forgot how long it took to drive to almost any point outside of Hazard. It might not be far as the crow flies, but her little car needed to stick to the mostly paved roads. Across one final bridge and ah, there it was. The remnants of what used to be a thriving company town showed itself alongside a hillside covered with gravestones.

Maggie stepped out of her car, pocketed her cell phone and keys, and set off up the rutted gravel drive. Her sturdy boots and jeans would protect her from snakes that liked hiding in the shaggy grass surrounding the oldest gravestones along the hilltop. It was after 8:30, and the sun would be falling behind the ridge in about twenty minutes, so she'd best hurry. Being in a graveyard after dark might not be the best idea. Just ask the foolhardy heroine of any 1980s teen movie.

Maggie walked quickly past the familiar stones. Neaces, Napiers, and Fugates dotted the landscape. But today her focus was on her great-grandmother: Rose Fraley Davis. Something had been tugging at the edge of Maggie's consciousness today, some kind of genealogical premonition that she was about to find something important. Reaching the hilltop, Maggie carefully navigated the crowded older stones, some so weather worn their carvings were lost. Each one represented a life, often cut short by a bare-bones existence.

When she came to the simple rounded stone she had discovered last week after hours of clearing fallen logs and brush, Maggie crouched down to touch the simple inscription.

Rose Davis
1891-1944

A shot of electricity coursed through Maggie's fingers and up her arm. She jerked, looking for an unseen sliver of glass, a wasp, or even a snake, but nothing unusual was in sight, just gently waving grasses in the summer breeze and shadows showing it was nearing twilight. Maggie touched the gravestone again, not certain what to expect, but she felt driven and...

Images of a wooden shack, a steaming iron pot over a fire, and nearly empty flour sacks all rushed through Maggie's mind. She shook her head to clear it only to see a man with a coal-blackened face and children with bare feet showing beneath too short overalls staring back at her.

This wasn't right, wasn't... Maggie sank to the ground not caring that grass wedged under her fingernails and stained her palms or that small rocks dug through her jeans to dent her knees.

. . . .

Maggie looked down to see she wore a blue flowered cotton dress. She was holding a cluster of honeysuckle, and a handsome young man with sparkling blue eyes and jet black hair stood grinning beside her. She accepted his hand and let him lead her down a courthouse hallway to where a bored clerk nodded for them to enter the judge's chambers. A stern looking justice of the peace gestured for them to come forward and then began speaking. "Do you, Henry Scotland Davis, take Rose Leotis Fraley as your wife? To have and to hold, from this day forward? For better. For worse. For richer. For poorer. In sickness and in health, 'til death do you part?"

Maggie's head spun, and she was running up a snowy hillside with Henry, plopping onto a battered metal tray then flying down the slope past thin trees and rock outcroppings until they landed in a heap at the bottom, laughing at this rare winter treat. Children ran after them, her younger brothers and sisters begging for a chance to sled down the hill. Henry helped her to her feet and stole a quick kiss before running off with the clamoring young'ins.

Another spin and Maggie seized with pain. She felt as if she might split apart, so she grabbed blindly at the hands supporting her. *A boy, a boy for my Henry,* she prayed, and a moment later she heard the gasp and squeak of a baby's first cry. Her granny wrapped the child in a cloth and handed Maggie her first daughter. *Pearl.* Contentment swirled through Maggie as she gazed down at the dark-haired infant who was already rooting for her breast.

The air shimmered and lightened as Henry's dirty face came into view, trudging along with the other men as they spilled out of the mine's entrance. The miners pushed deeper into the mountain every day, digging out coal so they might feed their families with food from the company store. Maggie stayed nervous with worry over Henry doing such dangerous, back-breaking work, but how else was he to earn a living in these hills?

Steam clouded Maggie's vision as she stirred a large cauldron simmering over a fire. A community butchering meant that the family would eat better for a while, and she'd been fortunate enough to obtain the hog's head. Her arms ached, but her spirits rose alongside the scent of cooking meat. That smell meant everyone's bellies would be full tonight.

Maggie blinked, and she was sitting in a rocking chair, holding a child whose chest rose and fell along with the ticking of the clock during the night. He didn't cry, didn't have the strength to move his limbs. Barely twelve days old and the ribs beneath his ashen skin were sharpening by the hour. Virgil would take but a few swallows of milk before turning his head away to drift to sleep. Maggie's chest ached less every day as her milk dried, although her heart ached more. As dawn crept over the mountain that morning, Virgil drew the last breath of his too short life.

Maggie's rocking chair creaked as she sat stringing beans for supper. She gazed out the open door as the little girls played hopscotch in the dirt, Lora Mae and Mary Magdalene, with Sam toddling along behind his sisters. She reckoned Sam might be her last child. Carrying twelve babies over the last twenty years had worn her out. Now some of her babies had babies, and she was right glad to be there to hold them in her arms.

Cold February wind blasted the north side of the house as coughs racked Maggie's body. Lord, these last few years had been hard. The phlegm in her chest rattled. Breathing became agony.

Then breath came no more.

· ·

Maggie woke with a jolt, gasping in a deep breath. She wiped her hands on her jeans, pulled her phone out of her pocket, and saw that it was not quite 9:00 p.m. Golden light still clung to the hillside as the sun moved westward. She hadn't spent more than ten minutes on the hilltop, but she'd experienced decades. She had *been* there, inhabiting Rose's life as she married, laughed, gave birth, rejoiced, mourned, and died.

Maggie began slowly walking down the hill. It was time to go back to her life, to 2019. Back to paved roads and GPS that would guide her out of the hills and hollers her grandparents had known by heart. Back to her family research where clicking a few keys found proof of the events in her ancestors' lives. She'd fallen asleep on the hillside, and her mind had taken all those discoveries, conjuring a *very* vivid dream of what might have been Rose's life.

As Maggie reached her car in the dusky light, the smell of honeysuckle wafted over her and laughter rang across the hills. It might all feel long ago, but the past had never been closer.

Part Three

· · · · · · · · · · · · ● · ● · · · · · · · ·

Pull up a chair... if you ain't too scared.

(Stories 2,501 words or longer)

If your landlord insists an antique stays

with the house, there's a reason.

Great Uncle's Rocker

By Jeanne G'Fellers

Genre: Paranormal

Keywords: haunting, West Virginia, coal country, family, ghost

CW: nightmares, illness

In 2014, I landed a job teaching English Language Arts for McDowell County, West Virginia, schools, in the heart of coal country, U.S.A. While the people of McDowell County and Welch, the county seat, were as welcoming and friendly as they come, the county was, and still is, poverty-stricken, and I had great difficulty finding acceptable housing as a result. It wasn't that I was picky, but I did have certain requirements: three bedrooms, two bathrooms, and things like floors that weren't rotten and a roof that didn't leak. Oh, and no flooding. I insisted on a home above the floodplain because McDowell County suffers regular flooding events and has experienced devastating floods in the past.

This wasn't my ideal job location, I'll admit, but it was a job, and after a disastrous teaching experience in Charlotte, North Carolina, the year before, I needed to be somewhere my accent and mannerisms weren't going to be openly and frequently ridiculed, and that place was in deep Appalachia.

It took me almost three months, an extended one-star motel stay, and ten eight-hour weekly commutes to find suitable housing, and this came via word of mouth. Mrs. Tonz, a science teacher, had recently purchased a home just over the county line, located on higher, safer ground. She was moving from a rental, and the landlord, John, was a Welch native, but he lived and worked in Washington D.C.. He owned several houses in Welch that he'd refurbished and rented at reasonable rates to professionals, meaning educators and medical staff, few of us McDowell County natives, who had chosen to work there. It was his way of paying back, of giving homage to his roots.

The historic four-bedroom home had been split into a duplex, each side measuring a good 1200 square feet. With only two bedrooms in our potential rental, it wasn't exactly what I was looking for, but Mrs. Tonz said the place was not only clean but also above the flood plain, so I had to take a look.

And she was correct. The available side of the duplex was nicely equipped, and the renovations had kept true to the house's character, including the original fireplace with blue hand-glazed tiles and its original mirror. There was even an old coal burner in the firebox. It no longer functioned, but it added a feel of originality to the house.

We'll take it, I said in my email to the owner. My sons could sleep upstairs in the bedrooms, and my spouse, Ara, and I would sleep downstairs in the living room in our recliners or on the couch until we figured out something better.

Excellent, John wrote back. *Electricity, water, and trash pickup are included in the rent, but there's one thing. The rocking chair in the corner of the living room was my great uncle's, so it stays in the house since both were his. I hope you can understand the sentimental value.*

"O...kay." I remember saying this aloud when I read his response. It was a beautiful old rocker, too low and delicate for any of us to sit in, so we'd use it as a decorative piece right where it sat in the corner by the window. I assured him that we'd take care of the rocker and overnighted him the deposit the very next day while my family finished packing down in Tennessee. We were going to be together again, see each other on a daily basis. That was most important.

I went to the house during the week before the move to drop off some framed art we didn't want broken during the transition. Once the art was safely tucked into the living room closet, I walked the house, upstairs and down, pleased by my stroke of luck. It was a very nice home. And the monthly rent, especially with the utilities included, was an excellent deal. It might not be exactly what we'd wanted, but in a place where the pickings were slim, this was a fine option indeed. "Nice house." I smiled when my voice echoed across the lower floor then turned toward the kitchen, ready to begin this new chapter in my family's life.

I shut off the kitchen light then walked to the living room to stand in the front doorway, taking a final look. The living room light turned off before I touched the switch. It shut off on its own accord. "Well now." I examined the switch cover to discover it was a unique combination of light and remote for the room's ceiling fan. It was also removable. That was the problem, I was certain. Bad batteries or a loose connection. I flipped the switch then left, thinking no more about it.

In early November, we moved into our half of the duplex and met our elusive neighbor, who managed a local medical office. It was one of only three times we ever saw her. This was a very quiet neighborhood but only because there were so many abandoned homes. Perhaps this requires some context. McDowell County, West Virginia, in its heyday, had a population of approximately 250,000 people. This was before the area's coal industry declined and people moved to where the jobs were, reducing the county population to under 25,000. That's a ninety percent drop, and those who left widely abandoned their homes and businesses. Immediately behind our home stood a boarded up two-story house, and catty corner from it stood a once proud yellow brick house, or what was left of it. It'd burned nearly to the ground a few years before we arrived. Across from our duplex and down the hill sat an abandoned home, while looking out our front door, left and across the street stood a brick shell that had once been a three story house. The roof was good, but every window was missing, frame, sash, and all, perhaps salvaged to make another home livable, but no one seemed to know for certain.

Once we'd settled into our new home, our lives returned to normal. Work. School. Ara is retired military, so she stayed home most days. Everything was like it had been... except for those lights. We had remote wall-mounted switch combinations in four rooms: the living room, dining room, and both bedrooms.

That said, the on and off again light problem wasn't limited to those spaces. The lights could turn off and on at seeming random in any room. Bathrooms. Upstairs hall. Even the pantry.

"It turned back on." Our eldest son pointed to the space beneath the pantry door. The light was shining, but the last person who'd been in there, me, had shut it off not ten minutes before.

"Seriously?" I turned just in time to see the light cut off again. "We've got wiring issues."

"You think?" Our younger son popped his head into the kitchen from the stairwell. "The light in my room cuts on and off at least twice a night."

"Living room too," I said. "Dead of night most times." I contacted the landlord the next day, and he sent his local handyman to check for a problem.

"Don't know what to tell you." The handyman told me late the next afternoon once he'd checked every light switch and the main box. "Everything's fine."

"But..."

"Maybe it's the ghost." He gathered his tools and left without saying more.

"Ghost?" Ara stared after him.

"He's joking." I dropped into the recliner and raised the footrest. "I'll ask Mrs. Tonz tomorrow."

'Please do." Ara peered warily at the ceiling fan while I began grading papers. I didn't have time for ghosts. I had seventy-four sixth and seventh graders who needed their writing assignments graded by tomorrow.

. . . .

I did as I said and asked Mrs. Tonz about the lights after a faculty meeting the next afternoon.

"We always said it was the ghost." She shrugged. "John had two different electrical contractors up from Bluefield to check the wiring while we were living there, but they never found anything." She gathered her papers and headed for the doorway. "Nice house, isn't it?"

"Yes, it is." The science teacher had said ghost too, but the house was indeed nice... ghost aside.

· ·

By January, the light play had become a normal happening for us. It occurred at random times but always at least once per night in the living room and usually around three a.m., which wouldn't have been bothersome aside from the fact Ara and I slept there. I solved the problem by keeping the remote on the table behind the couch so I could easily reach it, but the one night I forgot... "Can you just turn it off?" I said this half-awake out of frustration and was in mid-stand to retrieve the remote when the light shut off! "Thank you." What else was I supposed to say?

After that night it was more than just the lights. It was footsteps and shadows too. Someone or something walked the wooden stairs day and night, but the steps always faded before they reached the top or bottom landings. Our cats would sit and watch whoever was walking, but they didn't seem afraid, so we simply watched them watching. The shadows were far more disconcerting, but they definitely weren't coming from outside since we had so few neighbors. Besides, shadows inside the pantry under the staircase shouldn't have been possible, but there they were. We'd see the light come on and then a shadow that looked to be browsing the pantry shelves.

By February, we were experiencing sudden temperature changes and odd breezes in the living room. They often rose from behind our recliners near the window where John's great uncle's rocking chair sat. The cold would brush our faces then disappear. Yes, it was winter and the house was a century old, but it had been completely updated, and the heating system was more than sufficient.

We replaced the batteries in the fans' remotes numerous times, but nothing changed. "Let's take the batteries out of the one in the living room," Ara suggested one night, and we did, but the light still came on at three a.m.

Lights, steps, shadows, breezes, and cold spots. If we had a ghost, and by this point we knew we did, at least we had a benevolent one. Still, I wondered about that chair. It still sat in the corner, and we kept it dusted, but the cats avoided it when they'd sit and climb on everything else they could reach in the house.

. . . .

On Saint Patrick's Day, 2015, our world turned upside down. The chronic illness I'd been managing for a decade reared its head like never before, and I ended up in the hospital twice in one week, the second time in ICU. I was slow to recover after my release, so I took medical leave from work for the remainder of the school year. The ghost did all his usual tricks while I convalesced, but now I was there to see it all. We were definitely being haunted. Still, no one in our larger family believed us until my mother came to visit in early May.

"Why'd the light cut on?" she asked. It was midday, and we were sitting in the sunlit living room.

"The ghost," I mumbled, and Ara agreed.

Mom gave us an uh-huh look then went back to her reading until the cats drew her attention a few minutes later. "Is someone on the stairs?" She could see up the steep stairwell from her chair. "I thought I heard footsteps."

"The ghost," I repeated.

Mom watched the cats for a while then looked toward the kitchen. "I thought the boys were upstairs."

"They are," said Ara. "The ghost is in the kitchen."

She tried to shake this off and returned to her book only to shiver a few minutes later. "There's a draft in here."

"Ghost," I said. She ignored me, but at three a.m. when we were all trying to sleep in the living room and the overhead light turned on, she couldn't deny it any longer.

"You have a ghost. Not a bad one. A little mischievous given the time, but a ghost." The overhead light shut off again as if to agree. "Thank you," she mumbled, and we all went back to sleep.

Now the sight, or at least a minor version of it, runs in our family. My mother and I dream of things that might happen, especially deaths, and sadly, our dreams sometimes come true shortly thereafter. But an active haunting? I hadn't dealt with one until then.

· · · · · · · · · · ●●●●●●●●●●●● · · · · · · · · · ·

By June, it'd become clear that my health would never allow me to return to a classroom, so we made plans to return to Tennessee when our lease ran out. I was going to miss my students and colleagues, but I knew there was little I could do about the situation, and Tennessee was home. Our family was there, so we searched for a new rental, scheduled movers, and began packing.

"Put that rocker in the upstairs hall closet," I told my elder son in early September, a good six weeks before moving day. I wanted to assure that the chair with its great-uncle attachment didn't come with us when we moved, and the best way to do so was to put it somewhere safely out of the movers' sight. Yes, I'd made the connection between that chair and the ghost by that point. Why else would John have insisted that such a beautiful antique be left in his rental property?

The chair went in the closet, and we returned to packing, but that night my dreams were restless. I dreamt of shadows wandering the house, of someone looking for something, of frustration and growing anger, and twice I startled awake.

The cold breezes became icy, and the shadows grew darker and longer during the next week. My dreams were much the same when I managed to sleep. Looking. Searching. Restless. Our cats hid whenever steps descended the stairs to the living room, and our Siamese bristled when a shadow crossed the room late one evening. We were living amid a disarray of half-packed boxes and I was sick, I told myself. That was all.

"He's angry," said Ara one evening when the cold air brushed her face.

"Who?"

"John's great uncle."

"Why?" I thought he'd be happy we were leaving. I knew I was by that point. The house was crowded, and I had to crawl up the stairs on my hands and knees to reach the full bath. My illness had complicated everything, and I sometimes couldn't discern my body's messages from my surroundings. My skin frequently prickled for no apparent reason, and I stayed on edge, plagued by strange dreams. "Is he mad we're going or about his chair?"

"Both maybe? I don't know. But I think he's mad either way." Ara returned to her book.

That night my dreams were worse than ever. Searching. Looking. Angry. Upset. I tossed and turned on the couch, all but rolling off twice, trying to find the rest I desperately needed to function on any meaningful level the next day. The overhead light turned on and off at least a half-dozen times, and I heard mumbling behind the couch that I dismissed as one of the cats.

Around four in the morning, I finally slept soundly until I heard someone yelling at me and felt that same icy breeze cross my face. *Don't open your eyes.* But of course I did because I had to, because— A shadow stood over me, bent at the waist. I could just make out his features – a short, gray-haired man wearing glasses. He looked outraged, and I heard his voice clear as day though his mouth never moved.

"I want my chair!"

I sat up and the shadow, along with the breeze, disappeared. Needless to say, I didn't sleep any more that night and was a general mess when my younger son came down for breakfast three hours later. "Get that rocker out of the closet and set it in the upstairs landing." I told him. "We'll put a sign on it so the movers won't load it."

"After breakfast." He turned toward the kitchen.

"No. Now!"

"Okay. Sure, Mom." He bounded up the stairs, and I heard him move the chair to the landing. I relaxed after that and returned to the couch, where I slept peacefully until the early afternoon.

Things returned to what was normal for that house afterward. Footsteps and shadows, cold spots and light play, but no one invaded my dreams to yell at me. Peace had returned. John's great uncle had his chair back, and all was good with the world.

"There's a rocker at the top of the stairs with a sign on it. It stays here." I was emphatic about this when the movers arrived, and I double checked that they hadn't loaded the rocker by mistake before I'd let them close the moving van.

We moved away from Welch, West Virginia, in October 2015, returning to Tennessee and our family, and that rocker and John's great uncle remained in Welch so he can haunt whoever lives there now, but heaven help them if they ever try to move that chair.

Hush, young lady. Such panic is bad

for your delicate sensibilities.

Causing a Scene

By Anne G'Fellers-Mason

Genre: Horror, Paranormal

Keywords: ghosts, family, murder, crime, small town

CW: serial killer, mass murder

L ittle Alice Keefhaver was not the first ghost Sadie Baxter had ever seen. Her father had met her at school the morning the mine collapsed, trying to tell her something, but there were no sounds coming from his lips, only silent words. Little Alice Keefhaver didn't try to speak, rather, she pointed toward the house where she slept with her mother, father, three sisters, and one brother, all dead. The bloody axe that had done the deed was still sitting by the back door.

It wasn't so unusual for little Alice to be silent. She was the youngest of the Keefhaver clan and very shy. It was odd for her to be alone, though, and it was definitely odd that none of the Keefhavers were at school. Mrs. Keefhaver ran her family like a factory, and her five children were *always* at school.

It was the mid-day break, and Sadie was out in the school yard. Some children went home to eat, others ate in the school yard. Sadie usually went to the library. But earlier that week the library had developed a distinctive odor. It was either a dead mouse or an egg intentionally placed by one of the Fleenor brothers. Mr. Hardy hadn't figured out which yet, and the smell remained.

Sadie was walking through the yard, ham biscuit in one hand and a book in the other when she saw a flash of white from the corner of her eye. She lowered her book and looked across the yard to see little Alice standing on the other side of the fence. She appeared to be wearing her nightgown. Sadie walked straight to her. "You playing hooky, little Alice?" The girl didn't reply, which again, wasn't odd. "Your whole family playing hooky?" No response. "Your mama out of town or something? She finds out y'all laid low, she'll bust your britches." Silence. "Why are you in your nightgown? No one at home would dress you?"

Little Alice turned her body ever so slowly, her left hand rising and pointing back to the Keefhaver house. It was only a block down the street, and you could just make out the top of the house sticking above the trees. She pointed straight up to the attic, her eyes never leaving Sadie's. There was no emotion in those eyes. No shyness, no fear, no sleepiness, nothing. Sadie felt uneasy, and her throat clenched tight. The part of her lunch she'd eaten felt like a stone in her gut, and she wasn't interested in the rest of her biscuit. She felt cold all over, just like she had when her father had met her here two years ago.

"Oh no." Sadie turned her head to see who else was in the schoolyard, who else was nearby. When she looked back, little Alice was gone. A part of Sadie had known she would be, but Sadie walked straight up to the nearest kid, Clara Brownlow, anyway.

"Did you see little Alice just now?"

Clara gave her a funny look. "No. None of the Keefhavers are here today. Must be sick, or dead or somethin'," she laughed. Sadie dropped her biscuit and headed for the school gate. "Where are you going?" Clara called after her.

"I have to go. Tell Miss Smith I'm sick or something."

"I'll tell her you're crazy!" Clara shouted.

That wasn't the first or last time someone would call Sadie crazy.

They'd called her crazy since the mine accident, since the day her father died. They called her crazy for seeing him that morning in the school yard, when he was already dead underground, and they also called her crazy because she knew the truth. The mine collapse was no accident. Her father had caused it on purpose. He'd killed himself. Maybe that's what he was trying to tell her that morning? Maybe that's what he'd tried to tell her the night before when he'd come into her bedroom and stood at the foot of her bed? He'd been alive then, sure enough, but he still hadn't felt right. Sadie's father never checked on his children. He was not a man of outward emotion, but his sadness filled the room that night. The creak of the door had alerted Sadie to his presence. She'd woken, but she hadn't sat up, hadn't looked at him. She'd just felt him and all his sadness. Her father had sighed, a sigh a drowning man might make before giving in to his fate, then he'd left the room.

Sadie wished she was a better lip, or better yet, a mind reader.

And she wished she was a better meanderer. When she thought, she tended to walk in a straight line, and that is how Miss Smith caught her on the way to the Keefhaver house.

"And where are you off to, young lady? The mid-day break is almost through."

"I'm going home, Miss Smith, I don't feel so good."

"You don't feel so *well*. None of your tricks, Sadie Baxter, back to school."

Protesting wasn't an option. Sadie resigned herself, turned and headed back the other way. She passed Little Alice standing there in the road on the way back. The girl regarded her with silence. She hoped the ghost would be forgiving.

When the school day was finally done, Sadie tore out the door. Her school bag was a bit heavier with extra reading, a punishment for her distracted state all afternoon, but it wasn't going to slow her down. Even before she left the schoolyard, Sadie could tell the town had changed. Everyone was standing outside, looking at the Keefhaver house. Everyone was talking, and there was a large crowd down the street.

She made her way through the crowd, getting as close as she could to the house. The Sheriff was there. He and the town doctor were standing on the porch while a group of deputies tried to keep the crowd back. The house looked normal enough from the outside, but it certainly didn't feel right. Sadie walked around the house from the street as best she could. It felt wrong from all angles, and she could just catch a glimpse of something shiny by the back door, a glint of sun on metal.

By the time she made it back to the front of the house, the crowd was larger. The coroner from the next town over came stumbling out onto the front porch. He ran to the edge and vomited, and the crowd went into fits. What was going on? "All right, that's enough, show's over!" Sheriff Wills announced. "Move on out! Go home! This isn't for decent folk."

Tom Young from the local paper, the *Milltown Times*, spoke up. "Is it true they're all dead, and they've lost their heads?"

"Who told you that?" Sheriff Wills had never been a good poker player.

"So it's true!" The crowd went into fits again.

Sadie looked to her left, and there was Little Alice, standing at the edge of the group. Sadie made her way over to the girl. She was still dressed in her nightgown, still silent and sullen. As soon as Sadie reached her, she pointed slowly to the top of the house where the attic was.

"Same thing happened over in Cloverdale," said Wandering Pete. Sadie gasped and looked up. Little Alice was gone, and there was Wandering Pete, leaning against a nearby fence. Sadie wasn't sure who he was talking to, but he wasn't always sure either. Wandering Pete walked the roads and rode the rails, taking work wherever he could find it in the region. He was sometimes gone for months at a time, but now he was back.

"Whole family, murdered in their beds, heads chopped clean off." Now he was talking to her. "What's this world coming to? Go on home, Sadie, this ain't a place for young ladies."

Sadie nodded and walked off. There was nothing more to be done now, but she knew Little Alice wasn't through with her yet.

At home that evening, Sadie's mother tried her best to keep the conversation on something, anything else. But that didn't work with Sadie's older brother. "Dick Wilkins said their heads were sitting on the dresser, just staring at their headless bodies."

Mother Baxter, their father's mother, spoke next. "I always thought the Keefhavers were good, Christian people. What kind of sin could they have committed to deserve this?"

"Sadie, how was your day?" her mother asked out of desperation.

Sadie shrugged and continued pushing her potatoes around her plate. She couldn't save her mother tonight. "I have a lot of studying to do. May I be excused?"

"Girl doesn't need to study, she needs to eat, put some meat on her bones, or she'll never get a husband," Grandmother remarked.

"I wonder who did it? Who butchered the Keefhavers?" Sadie's brother contemplated his question around a bite of pork.

Her mother sighed. It was going to be a long night. "Yes, Sadie, you may be excused."

"Coulda been Wandering Pete," her brother mused. "The guy's off his rocker."

"He's an honest man who fell on hard times, Cecil. Do not speak ill of him." Her mother was finally compelled to join their conversation.

"Probably that Eugene Muntz, never right in the head," Sadie's grandmother suggested.

"He was deprived of oxygen at birth, Mother Baxter. He'd never harm a fly."

"He did kill the family dog," Cecil pointed out.

"Eugene doesn't know his own strength," her mother defended.

That was the last Sadie heard as she climbed the steps to her room. She did try to study. The books were before her on the bed, the lamp was on, and occasionally she read a page or two. But her eyes kept looking to the foot of her bed, expecting to see Little Alice or maybe her father, she wasn't sure. That was how her mother caught her some hours later, just sitting there in the growing gloom, staring into space. "Sadie, are you all right?"

Sadie startled and looked up. "Yeah, I'm fine, just taking a break. My eyes were crossing." She rubbed her eyes and looked at the book before her. She was still on page five.

"Sadie..." her mother began, but she didn't finish. Her silence, however, contained whole paragraphs. She was worried, worried Sadie would become like before, go back to how she was when her father died.

Those had been hard months when Sadie had worked to discover the truth. First, it was obvious clues, like her father's will, the deed to the property, and his life insurance all stacked neatly at the top of his trunk. Other clues were less obvious, like the bird cage hidden in the shed, the yellow feathers Sadie found, and the tiny dropper next to the rat killer. Some clues were said by friends and coworkers at the funeral. They spoke of rumors that the mine had been fixing to close. The company was sure they'd scraped the hills dry, and they had new exploits. But the accident had kept them from reaching that final pocket, and since only one man had died, the man in charge, they'd cleaned up the accident and pressed on. It was only after the incident that the company had discovered a whole new cache. Then the mine had flourished, as had the town.

The puzzle had kept Sadie up at night. She barely ate and hardly slept. Her mother, lost in her own grief, didn't know what to do with her. Her brother ignored her, and Grandmother Baxter condemned her to hell. Sadie discovered the final piece of the puzzle late one night, while she was ransacking the house. There was no other word for it. In her manic state, she'd discovered a map hidden beneath a loose floorboard in her father's office. It was a map of the mine, of the cache her father thought was there but the company had yet to find. With the map were communications that the company was closing the mine, effective in two weeks. There was no way they'd reach the cache by then, not without a drastic step.

As best Sadie could figure, her father had bought a canary, poisoned it, and snuck it in to the mine that morning. He'd had everyone evacuated for a false gas leak, and then he'd stayed behind to knock the supports down around himself.

"He killed himself! Father killed himself!" she'd called out and woken the whole house. That'd been a rough night, a rough month, a rough year. The family still wasn't right, and knowing the truth hadn't made Sadie feel any better.

"Sadie?"

"I'm fine." Sadie startled again. "I'm just tired." I think I'll get some sleep. Goodnight" Sadie set her book aside and turned off the lamp, so her mother only lingered a moment before moving on.

Surprisingly, Sadie was able to find sleep, and she wasn't sure what time it was when the creak outside her door woke her. She sat up at once, expecting to see her father, but saw her older brother, sneaking out. "Where're you going?" she hissed into the darkness.

"Go back to sleep," he whispered.

"Tell me." Sadie climbed from her bed. "If you don't, I'll wake Grandmother Baxter."

"You wouldn't."

Sadie opened her mouth to speak, but her brother shushed her. "I'm meeting Dick at the Keefhaver house. We're sneaking in to see the crime scene."

"What about Sheriff Wills?"

"It's after two, so he's gotta be drunk by now."

This was a very true statement. "I'm coming with you."

"Suit yourself, just be quiet," her brother cautioned.

Sadie quickly put on her coat and grabbed her shoes.

Thirty minutes later, the two of them met Dick outside the large, white house. Cecil and Dick had been close friends since childhood. Last year, though, at the age of fifteen, Dick's father had put him to work in the mines. Cecil was still in school, and he was constantly trying to prove to Dick that he was brave, trying to repair the growing rift between them. It was never easy being the foreman's family, even after the foreman's death.

"Why'd you bring your crazy sister?"

Cecil shrugged. "She's fine."

"If you see any ghosts, keep your yap shut." Dick pointed a finger at Sadie, and she nodded. Dick Wilkins had never been worth arguing with.

Dick had already scouted the house and discovered an open window on the ground level at the back. Sadie paused as they approached, remembering the glint she'd seen earlier. "That's where they found the bloody axe," Dick told Cecil as they passed.

The three of them slipped silently into the house, which was still and dark. They moved carefully, walking through the kitchen and the parlor to the first-floor bedroom. The bed inside was stripped of all its bedding and there were two, distinctive red stains on the mattress. "This is where they found Mabel and Scout," said Dick. They'd been little Alice's older sisters.

"Where'd they find the heads?" Her brother asked in a tense voice.

Sadie left the boys to their gruesome tale, heading up the stairs to the second floor. She didn't look in the bedrooms because she knew what she'd see there. Instead, she moved on to the small staircase at the end of the hall, the one that led to the attic. Sadie wasn't sure what she was looking for, or why she was even there. The small window at the end of the attic pulled her forward, and she let herself be guided. The attic looked over the yard then the street. The moon shone down, and Sadie knew, knew someone else had looked out that window, someone not related to the Keefhaver family. "Is this where you waited?" she whispered into the dark. A sound caught her attention, and she turned, half-expecting an answer. It was only the scuttling of a mouse, nothing more, but as she turned, a flash of white caught her eye. There was a piece of paper sticking out from behind an old chest. Sadie bent down and picked it up, frowning when she saw it was a new map of the Southern Railway lines, only slightly crumpled. Why would that be in the attic?

Sadie took the map downstairs with her. Sheriff Wills would

never find it up there, so she left it in the kitchen, near the stove, in a somewhat noticeable place. She went to find the boys, giving them a terrible scare in the process. Dick screamed so hard he cried, and then he wanted to go home.

The next morning, the paper was full of the story. Keefhaver family of seven all dead, all slain in their beds. They'd all been killed the same way, beheaded by an axe that was later found by the backdoor. There were no other clues than that. Most curious of all, no one had woken up during the killings or put up a fight. Tom Young wondered if they'd been drugged. This was by far the worst crime to strike Milltown, and everyone wanted to know who'd done it. No one out of the ordinary was in town, save for a doctor from Boston who'd lodged with the Robinson family, but he'd left the day before for a medical conference. He had conferred briefly with Mr. Keefhaver on the street, and the two had seemed to share a most pleasant conversation.

The end of the article briefly mentioned identical murders had occurred in Cloverdale, Racine, and Simpsonville over the past ten years. Was this a terrifying new trend?

Sadie stewed over the article all day at school. She was glad it was Friday and that she had two days off. She'd need it for all the extra homework she kept accruing. But Sadie couldn't be expected to pay attention in class, not with so much happening around her. There was a reason Little Alice had visited after she was dead. There was a reason she was pointing to the attic. She had a message for Sadie, just like her father had. That map of the Southern lines was her message, but Sadie had to figure out what it meant.

After school, Sadie headed straight for the library, which had finally aired out. Mr. Hardy collected newspapers within a 1,000-mile radius and had them bound at the end of every year. They took up more space than the town's board was willing to provide shelves for, so they collected dust on the floor. Everyone told him to get rid of them, and no one ever touched them, so when Sadie asked to see them, he almost fell out of his chair.

Sadie worked through supper, sending a message home with her brother. Mr. Hardy let her stay past closing, thrilled someone was finally using his creations. In those pages, Sadie found more of the pieces to her puzzle. After the murders in Racine, a local doctor had wondered if there had been some sort of paralytic administered to the victims, keeping them sedated as they were murdered. Each time, there had been no one new or suspicious hanging about the families. Someone local had been convicted of the murders, someone convenient, easy, someone it didn't take a lot of evidence to convict.

The murders in Cloverdale and Racine had happened five years ago. Between the two families, there had been eleven deaths. Four in one family, seven in another. Simpsonville had happened two years ago, and there had been eleven deaths, two families in the same household. "Seven Keefhavers," Sadie whispered.

When it started getting dark, Mr. Hardy encouraged Sadie to leave, but he told her to come back tomorrow if she wanted. As she walked home, she turned the new information over in her mind. "Seven Keefhavers. Seven Keefhavers." A group of men stood outside the Muntz house, and Sadie slowed her steps as she approached.

Just then, the front door banged open, and Sheriff Wills stepped out, dragging a screaming Eugene with him. Mrs. Muntz was right behind them. "You can't take my boy! He didn't do it!"

"We have to question him, Gladys, you know that," the Sheriff insisted, and Eugene wailed incoherently.

"He was here with me all night! Go question Wandering Pete!"

"Pete spent the night at the church, preacher can vouch for him."

"I can vouch for my boy!"

"Everyone knows you take ether to help you sleep, Gladys. You're dead to the world, and your boy wanders the streets."

"He'd never hurt a soul!"

"He strangled your hound with his bare hands!"

Eugene wailed louder, and Mrs. Muntz reached for him. "It's all right, Eugene, these men just want to ask you some questions. Be brave for your mama! You'll be all right!"

"We'll bring him back in the morning." Sheriff Wills passed Eugene off to some of his men and they loaded him into the wagon.

Sadie hurried on, trying not to seem conspicuous. Poor Eugene. Poor Mrs. Muntz. Bits and pieces of the articles she'd read bounced in her head. They were already finding a scapegoat, just like in the other towns. It was a pattern. "Seven Keefhavers," she whispered and then stopped. Four, four more people had to die. The killer worked in elevens. The killer would strike again soon.

Sadie didn't sleep that night. She returned to the Keefhaver house on her own when it was well past three in the morning. The map of the Southern rails was still sitting where she'd left it in the kitchen. Sheriff Wills hadn't even noticed.

The next day, Sadie was back at the library early. Mr. Hardy was all too glad to set the newspaper volumes back on the table for her while she filled the notebook she'd brought, writing down every detail about the murders. What were the commonalities? It wasn't the families, save for the number of dead, but it was the location. The towns were all of similar size; they were all on the Southern line. The killer was following the rails. Sadie left the table and ran to the map at the front of the library. Her finger traced down, following the line, and she raced back to the table where she wrote the names of the nearest towns. She asked Mr. Hardy for any information he might have on them, and by lunch time, she'd narrowed it down to Pottsburg, only one hundred miles away. It made sense. Cloverdale and Racine were nearby.

Sadie returned the books, tucked her notebook under her arm, and walked home, knowing what she had to do. At home, she packed a small bag and collected her savings from the box hidden beneath her bed. She'd finished packing when her mother entered the room, her concern palpable. "People in town have been talking—"

The town needed a new hobby. Sadie put on her best face and turned to her mother. "Can I spend the night at Clara's?"

"Clara Brownlow's?" This caught her mother off guard. Clara and Sadie had been friends, once, in another life, before the mine collapsed.

"Yeah, Clara Brownlow's."

Her mother couldn't contain her smile, and Sadie almost felt guilty. "Of course. Have fun."

"We will," Sadie assured. That was all it took to get her down the stairs, out of the house, and on her way to the train station. She made a quick stop along the way to pay off Clara so she'd play along, and then she was on the next train to Pottsburg.

The train ride would take some time, but that was all right, Sadie needed time to figure out her next step. The only reported stranger in town had stayed with the Robinsons two days before the Keefhavers were killed. Why the Robinsons' house? Because it was the nicest lodging closest to the Depot. That's where Sadie needed to go when she got to Pottsburg, and lodging was the first question she asked the station master as she disembarked.

His answer led her to the Washington Hotel, slightly larger than the Robinsons' farm. The man at the front desk was wary of her, a young, single lady checking in by herself at such a late hour. Sadie explained she was there to surprise her uncle, who was in from Boston. He was a doctor on his way to a conference. She hadn't seen him in so long. Could she please leave a message for him? The man behind the counter checked her in without further question and took her message. "Uncle, I'm here to see you. I'd love to meet for breakfast. I have news for you from the Keefhavers in Milltown."

Once Sadie was locked inside her room, the absurdity of the situation almost overwhelmed her. What was she doing here? Hunches, she was playing hunches. What if she was forcing the pieces of the puzzle? What if they weren't meant to go together? But the clerk had seemed to know the man Sadie was describing, her false uncle. What if there was a doctor from Boston staying here? What if he was the murderer? What if he wasn't? What would Sadie do in either case, and how would she prove it? She'd need an answer by morning, but she had the rest of the night to think. But Sadie hadn't slept in nights, and her body finally forced its needs on her.

Sadie woke to thin streams of light sifting through the curtains, early light. It'd soon be time for breakfast, so she went to sit up but found she couldn't move. Sleep still held her fast, so she tried to wriggle her fingers or shake her feet, to stretch, but she could do none of those things. She was frozen, her limbs heavy and useless. Breathing even felt different, tighter. Her eyes went wide open in panic, and she could hear faint squeaks escaping her mouth.

"Don't panic. Breathe normally, makes it easier." A strange face stared down at her, smiling slightly. "It's your uncle. Don't you recognize me?"

Sadie tried desperately to move, but it was to no avail. "Calm down." The man sat in the bedside chair, watching. The minutes wore on, hours perhaps, and he simply watched her until she quit fighting. "I gave you less than the others, so you're more awake. You might even be able to speak with some effort. I must drug them, you see. It keeps them from fighting back, from screaming, creates less mess, cleaner cuts. One little prick at the bottom of the leg, that's all it takes."

"Who?" She managed to squeak out.

"I'm a doctor from Boston on his way to a medical conference. I am well respected and immediately to be trusted."

"Keefha..." Sadie struggled.

"The Keefhavers, yes, nice family. Mr. Keefhaver was extremely pleasant, told me all about his five children, told me where he lived. I checked out of the Robinsons' house and spent the next night in their attic. I have a way of getting into where I need to be, but so do you." The man leaned forward, and Sadie tried to flinch.

"Why?" she whispered.

The man sucked on his bottom lip. "I don't know. Because I can, perhaps? Because it's a new century, and men construct whole buildings that do nothing but kill people. Did you ever hear about H.H. Holmes and his work at the Columbian Exposition? Probably not. Milltown is very small. He was a doctor too, you know."

A tear trickled down Sadie's cheek, alarmingly warm when the rest of her felt so cold.

"I wondered if anyone would ever catch me, and here you are. I'd love to know how you figured me out, but not today." He leaned to the floor, and when he righted, Sadie saw a large syringe in his hand. He gave it a good flick, sending tiny droplets into the air. She whimpered, but she'd been trying to scream.

"I'm actually glad you found me. Seeing as you're a woman, I won't have to kill you. No one will believe your story. You know I'm right."

Sadie knew. She knew all too well.

"You had a case of the hysterics, a mood swing, a bad dream. Ma'am, please, calm down, you're causing a scene." The man chuckled, clearly pleased with himself. "This dose will give you a good sleep, and when you wake, you won't remember this, not really. In time, you'll convince yourself it was all a dream." He leaned toward her, needle poised and ready. Sadie tensed internally, even though her muscles could not physically respond. "I wonder if that's what my victims think when they see me standing over them. Am I a bad dream that spilled over into the waking world?" He mulled this over before returning to his task. "I am glad I don't have to kill you. I think the world is much more interesting with you in it."

Sadie didn't feel the needle's prick, but sleep came heavy and fast. There was nothing but darkness and silence.

Two days later, Sadie was back home in Milltown. The weekend and its events were a blur. Clara Brownlow had ratted her out, and Sadie thought she should ask for her money back. Her mother's hunt through town had taken her to the depot, where the station master shared what he knew. All of this had culminated in Sadie's mother finding her near comatose in a Pottsburg hotel bed. Her mother was too mad to speak to her, which was fine since Sadie didn't know what to tell her anyhow.

The drug faded from Sadie's system, but she remained fatigued. She didn't want to sleep, but she didn't want to move either. Sadie didn't know if she'd let Little Alice down or not, but she hadn't seen the ghost since that first day, so maybe all was forgiven.

Sadie lay on the bed, watching the hands tick on her bedside clock. Mother Baxter occasionally passed her room, muttering about asylums and basements with good locks, but she never crossed the threshold. Eventually, Sadie heard someone enter the room, and her brother walked around the bed to stand before her.

"Are you dead?"

"No."

"Good." He fidgeted. "Father died. Mother can't lose you too." With that, her brother turned and left the room. Sadie hadn't responded but she knew he was right, and some hours later, she had another visitor.

Sadie rolled over and curled into her mother's side when she sat on the bed, but they didn't say anything for the longest time.

"Your father came to me, too, on the day he died," her mother said. "It was that night. I was sitting on our bed, crying, and suddenly he was there. The bed dipped, and I felt his hand on my leg, his breath on my neck, his cheek against mine."

Sadie curled tighter against her mother. "What do you think he was trying to tell me?"

Her mother kissed her forehead and spoke without hesitation. "That he loved you more than life."

Sadie could live with this, whether it was true or not.

Her mother stroked her hair. "Did you find any answers in Pottsburg?"

"No. Only a bad dream."

Years passed. Sadie graduated high school and was able to obtain entry into a nearby college. Her passion was journalism, and she got a position with the school paper, which turned into an internship with the local newspaper. The publisher was so impressed with her work, he used his connections to get her hired by a larger paper several towns over. In ten years' time, Sadie was far from Milltown.

She was waiting at the station for a train to take her to the scene of an interesting murder. The police were calling it a crime of passion, but Sadie knew it wasn't that simple. She was good at investigative journalism, good at solving puzzles. Over the years, she still remembered Little Alice, and though she couldn't remember what happened in Pottsburg, she remembered the pattern. The killer had struck once more over the years but had been silent since that time. Murders happened, but none quite like the beheadings that followed the railroad line.

Sadie scribbled in her notebook, consumed by her newest case, when a voice spoke from above. "May I join you?" Sadie didn't look up, but nodded her head and a gentleman sat beside her. "Press, I see."

Sadie looked at her traveling bag and realized her press tag was sticking out. "Yes." She tucked it back in.

"You don't see many women journalists."

"There's more and more of us every day." This was her standard reply, one that was finally coming true.

A train whistle sounded from down the tracks. "I believe that's my train," the gentleman rose.

Sadie finally looked up to see his face. It looked familiar, but she couldn't place it. "I'm sorry, have we met?"

"I've been told I have a familiar face."

No, it was something else, and Sadie struggled to figure out exactly what as the train pulled into the station.

"You look exactly the same," said the man. "I was right; the world is much more interesting with you in it."

Sadie's heart dropped into her stomach when small snippets of the Pottsburg hotel returned. That voice! She couldn't forget that voice no matter how much she buried it in her mind, and it still haunted her dreams. Here he stood while Eugene Muntz rotted in jail. Here he stood while Mrs. Muntz was long buried from an ether overdose. Here he stood, ten years older when Little Alice would never age another day.

The train doors opened, and the platform filled with people. Sadie stood, but the man disappeared into the crowd. She tracked him as best she could, and when she climbed onto a luggage cart, she saw him disappear into the car of a Southbound train.

Sadie hopped down and ran for the nearest attendant, her blood thrumming in her veins. "Please, you have to help, there's a man on that train, a known killer. I believe he's going to strike again!" Sadie grabbed the attendant's arm, but he quickly shook off her hold.

"Ma'am, please calm down. You're causing a scene."

Histories, haints, and horrors often intertwine.

The Salt Creek Valley Monkey Dog

By Edward Karshner

Genre: Historical Magical Realism, Paranormal

Keywords: monster, Yahoo, Tecumseh, Shawnee,

Native Americans, Ohio, magic, 18th century

CW: violence, mild gore, murder

These being the secret recollections of The Honorable Daniel Karshner, woodsman, hunter, and, most recently, esteemed member of the Ohio General Assembly— 1843.

Salt Creek Valley, Ohio Purchase Territory, 1791

I could smell the homesite before I saw it— burnt wood and cooked meat. In the hollow, the cabin, corral, and barn smoldered. My legs went weak, so I dropped to a knee to watch the shadows playing funny in the trees as the gloaming slowly slipped away. I was too late.

I made my way down, keeping to the trees and shadows until there were only stumps then stopped to listen. No voices, no sounds, only the sizzle of wood and flesh. My long rifle pointing the way, I walked past the heavy elm door, ripped from its leather hinges and tossed into the clearing then to the cabin, stopping at the threshold.

Three bodies: man, woman, and a child were stretched on the floor, relieved of their heads. They were barefoot, the bottoms of their feet dirty and tough. I couldn't stop looking, and when I finally pulled my eyes away, I couldn't stop seeing them.

I bent over, purging myself of the jerky and beans I'd eaten earlier then wiped my eyes with the back of my hand and studied the cabin. It was one room, long and narrow. I caught movement up front, by the back door, so I raised my rifle.

"Hold!" I hollered, more scared than angry, hoping he wouldn't know the difference. "What happened here? Who are you?"

Backlit by the fading day, in the door stood a tall man in a gray frock coat and a floppy hat. He kept to the shadows, but I could see his beard shine white. My finger tightened on the trigger, but he was gone, out the door, and I feared to waste the shot.

With prudence, I followed him outside, rifle at the ready, but saw no gray man. The hill behind the cabin was thickly wooded and steep, so I moved to the right, down a trail toward the stables. The fire had collapsed the roof, but I could see the charred rumps of two horses, Belgians, both eviscerated, their insides strewn along the path that ran to the pasture.

The man rose up on me like a shadow from the ground. I froze as he clasped one hand behind my head and the other under my chin. My rifle discharged into the ground, but the man didn't so much as flinch. His breath rustled my beard, and his nose pressed against my ear.

"*Hwaet*," he said.

I felt heavy with dread and ashamed for being caught. "Beg your pardon?"

"Listen."

I regained my senses, pulled my knife, going for his guts, but again, he was gone. It was if he had never been there aside for his breath still in my ear. "Listen."

To what? They were all dead. Even the livestock. The carcasses of chickens and a turkey had been torn so as to look like gory stuffing from a pillow. I loaded my rifle and stood still, listening as I'd been told.

It was quiet, but not just silence. No, I was accustomed to the latter. This was other than the absence of noise. It was a void, the kind of nothing that portends evil, but you're drawn to follow it anyway.

In the fading light, near the pasture, I found deep tracks and blood leading toward the woods. I followed because it was my duty, what I'd been charged with.

I moved deeper into the woods, darkness folding around me like a cloak, and I took comfort from it. Most folks feared darkness, but I found simplicity in it. I knew that anything out there, in the dark, might mean me harm. Darkness set the rules, and that greased my actions. No second thoughts, just reaction.

Darkness brought a blessing of visceral violence against evil. Darkness made sense in those terms.

Night rolled up the homestead behind me, so I skirted along a ridge that hemmed me between the Salt Creek below and a thick forest of beech and elm to my right. The deeper I got in to the woods, the madder I became. I'd let that haint get the drop on me, let him get away after tearing up that family I was sent to protect. I could still hear it, "Listen." No, *it* would listen.

"We'll meet and settle up soon. You got my word," I said into the darkness.

I focused on the bloody tracks that pulled me deeper into the woods, my mind consumed with the reckoning I planned to dole out on that haint. Onward, then I realized I'd lost my way. The gory tracks lay in front of me, but I had no idea what was behind me. No idea where I was.

I felt adrift in a void amid a suspension in nothingness that wanted to pull me apart. I stopped walking and let my eyes adjust, listening.

Off to my right, I heard a grunt, a snort like a stag but lower, feeling it reverberate in my bones. The deep, guttural sound rode up my legs and spine to ring my ears.

I moved toward the sound on my knees until I was within the tree line then stood slowly, keeping to the shadows cast by hoary sycamores. My long rifle was tucked close to my side, beneath my arm pit, and my thumb hovered on the hammer. I was fixed to send a pure silver .48 caliber ball right into that haint that would blow him back to Hell.

Now he would listen.

As I moved closer, I could feel the noise in my chest. I was upon it, so I took up a firing position behind a downed beech tree just as the moon slipped from behind a cloud, illuminating the small clearing. I could see two heads on the ground, their eyes and mouths wide open. The boy's dead eyes seemed to notice me. I looked away, moved to my right then rose and aimed, but it weren't no haint.

It was as big as a horse, thick through the shoulders, and covered in dirty, white fur that cast green in the moonlight. Its back legs were thick and stiff like an elephant's, but the front legs were longer, stronger. The creature was on all fours, leaning against a tree. It put me in mind of a cross between a monkey and a dog, although of a physical immensity I'd never encountered.

At the click of my rifle, the Monkey Dog turned its head, the body following awkwardly. Its face was flat and hairless, and I could not discern its eyes, only a dark abyss under a ridged brow and a fall of curly hair. It pivoted on its hind quarters and pushed itself with one of its front arms, the other holding the head of the man, which the creature looked to have been gnawing on like an apple.

We faced each other, separated by a space of some thirty yards, and it roared the same deep vibration that had brought me to it. The Monkey Dog dropped the head and propelled itself toward me by placing its arms out front and hopping its stiff back legs like a rabbit.

For the second time that night, I froze. I faced that critter in a solid firing stance, rifle cocked and at my shoulder. It was lined up in my sights, but I couldn't move.

The Monkey Dog raised up, snorted, and took a long hop forward, its mouth wide open. My rifle discharged, and I heard a scream like a goat being butchered as time froze in the smoke of my weapon. I dropped the rifle and reached for the twin pistols, also loaded with pure German silver, that were tucked in my belt. Before I could pull, the smoke faded, and I was alone in the clearing except for the three heads now looking away from me. My ears rang from my shot, but I could see the forest snap back into place as the Monkey Dog tore, hell bent, away from me.

I took up my long rifle to reload while off to my left a group of men entered, boldly and without stealth. They had no fear of me and showed little concern for the Monkey Dog, although their timing suggested they had witnessed the entire event. Judging from their dress, hair, and face decoration, they were Shawnee, which should have worried me but strangely didn't.

I reckoned that in my chase, I may very well have crossed into Indian Territory, though that was not my intention. I lowered the rifle and leaned on the barrel, my knees still a little weak.

The party fanned around me, silent, the men moving to my right, stepping over the heads. An older man with dramatic nose piercings and a long scar down his face approached me. We squared off as the others stopped moving.

"*Kwe-kwe*," I said, figuring a nice hello might ease the tension.

The old man peered at my rifle and pistols before he looked at me. "Long way from home."

We were going to talk, were we? I was concerned that giant critter might come back, and if it didn't, I intended to set out after it.

I removed my hat and took out the folded parchment I kept there. "My name is Daniel Karshner," I said loudly, hoping volume would convey boldness. "I am a surveyor for the Ohio Company and a commissioned agent of the United States of America." I unfolded the paper and handed it to the old man. "See? It's signed by the Great Chief George Washington."

He took the paper and studied it, obviously not a reader since his eyes locked on the entire document and his head moved to take in chunks, not words. He grunted, and a younger man stepped forward, catching the document when the old man passed it over his shoulder with a dismissive shrug.

"My name is Tecumseh," said the young man. "I am pleased to make your acquaintance."

I'd heard of Tecumseh, an impressive individual I'd been told. His face was calm but determined, his shoulders broad and thick like his head was resting on a log. And he read my document with interest.

"George Washington," he said, handing the paper back to me.

"That's right." I folded the paper and returned it to my hat.

"Do you know George Washington?" His words poured from his mouth as smooth and warm as fine English Brandy.

"No, sir. The General and I haven't had cause to meet."

"And, yet," Tecumseh said. "You carry his signed orders."

"Well, he's the chief."

Tecumseh cocked one brow.

"Executive." I dropped my hat onto my head. "Chief Executive."

He nodded.

"I mostly deal with the Secretary of State, Thomas Jefferson."

"Ah, the great polymath. We have heard of him as well."

I looked to the woods, to the ravine the Monkey Dog had descended into, anxious to get back to it. "I need to set out after that critter I was hunting."

"That would be ill advised," said Tecumseh.

"He's wounded. I intend to finish him."

Tecumseh and the old man exchanged a look, and the old man sighed deeply.

"The *Ya'kwahe*," Tecumseh said. "The *critter*, as you call it, is not wounded. Quite angry, I imagine."

I adjusted my hat and hooked a thumb in my belt, trying to figure a way out of this useless meeting.

"Please join us for a meal and hospitality." Tecumseh seemed to have sensed my reluctance. "We have much to discuss. Perhaps we could be of assistance to each other."

I let the invite roll around in my head. It was dark, and I was lost well within Indian Territory, so at the moment it was better to be friendly than committed. "I believe that is a fine idea indeed."

· ·

Hockhocking Hunting Grounds

Within the natural shelter of the large recess cave, Shawnee braves roasted fat rabbit over roaring fires and vegetables in the coals along the edge. There was laughter and singing. Tecumseh motioned me to sit on a ledge close to a small fire but away from the others working at our supper. I watched him, a confident leader of men, briefly join a small group tending to rabbit skins. They exchanged words and a hardy laugh then Tecumseh returned with two tin cups of cold, clear water from the pool that collected under a nearby waterfall.

"Thank ye." I nodded.

He sat beside me, contented as he watched his men at their industry.

I reached into my pack and took out my crock of corn liquor, splashing a nip in my cup before I offered the crock to Tecumseh.

"No." He held up his hand. "It is against my beliefs."

I nodded and corked my jimmy john. "I know some Methodists like that."

We sat for a bit, quiet, letting the night set the rhythm for our talk.

"What brings you into our territory, Daniel?" He finally asked.

This man was not likely to take favorably to obfuscation, but I still pondered his reasons. "Reports have come back that settlers in the Buffer Land have gone missing and, as I've seen recently, faired much worse."

"And your government believes it to be us? These," he nodded toward the cooking fires. "Blood thirsty savages?"

"What were all y'all doing out there this night?" I asked.

He faced me, rebuking me without a word until I remembered who I was talking to.

"No, sir. If'n they did, you'd be talking to Lieutenant Harrison and some Pennsylvania Militia about now."

"Then why send you?" Tecumseh asked.

That was a hard question with an easy answer, if a fellow was ready to hear. "I'm a hunter. I hunt monsters," I said, knowing how it sounded.

Tecumseh let silence fall between us again. "How have you lived?"

"Beg your pardon?"

"That 'critter' you saw. What did you call it?" He inquired.

"A Monkey Dog," I said. "That's what it looked like. I think it was a Yahoo. At least that's what Dan Boone called them."

"According to your belief, what is this 'Yahoo'? Tecumseh asked.

"The Fallen Ones, giants. Nephilim."

"How do you kill these fallen ones?"

At the Philosophical Hall in Philadelphia, the members of the American Philosophical Society had quizzed me on assorted haints, boogers, and hobgoblins. It was the final step before getting a field assignment, so I was fitful at being tested again.

"With this." I reached into my bag and pulled out a silver fork.

"Dinnerware?" Tecumseh wondered.

"No. Silver. Pure German silver. It once belonged to Martin Luther himself. Melted into shot, it'll send back to Hell anything from there."

"What is Hell?" Tecumseh asked.

I started to answer but stopped. Hospitality was one thing. Being interrogated on a secret mission was making me nervish.

"You called the *Ya'kwahe* a Yahoo like the great Boone. You say it is a Nephilim. It is none of these," Tecumseh said.

"Then, what is it?"

Tecumseh looked into the woods. "There are others like us, only they serve the Powers Below. They are powerful sorcerers, but there is only weakness in Evil, so Evil always requires a proxy." I took a drink from my cup, tasting the tart liquor in my water while Tecumseh took a moment to collect his thoughts. "The *Ya'kwahe* were once people, people like us. Some white. Some Indian. The Sorcerers captured them." He sipped from his cup. "These Sorcerers eat the brain. Not all of it, just the part that makes us human. Only the small part we share with the evil ones is left. What was once a human being reverts back to the root stock. They become *Ya'kwahe*, a naked bear, a soulless creature."

I thought back to that hairy booger from the clearing. It was hard to square what I had seen with a human being, and I said as much.

"You doubt me?" Tecumseh asked.

"I'm trying to rectify your words with my eyes, is all."

"You are a hunter?"

"Yes. We're called *Der Yaeger*."

"These men." He points around the camp. "We are called *Tipwiwe*. Witnesses. We also hunt these creatures."

"So we're on the same side." I put the fork back in my bag.

"Yes, but your rules, your beliefs, don't work here. You will get yourself killed. You must learn to think within this environment," Tecumseh offered.

"How?"

"You must learn the story."

I was fitful at being lectured too. "I got a story. My story." I showed him my German Bible.

He sighed then stood, dropping wood into the fire.

"When the Finisher, Manitou, created this," Tecumseh patted nearby sandstone, "he created our Grandmother, and she created us. Then, it was only human beings, our grandmother and her brother, Motshee Manitou. He was not a good spirit.

No, he was jealous of Grandmother." Tecumseh snapped a thick piece of wood and threw it into the fire. "This is often the case with brothers." He grew quiet, watching the fire with pained attention.

"So," Tecumseh straightened himself and pulled in a breath, expanding his massive chest, "Motshee Manitou created his own beings, the Powers Below, the Snake People. This was not good. As Motshee Manitou nursed a grievance against Grandmother, so did the Snake People. They looked on human beings with contempt. But our Grandmother loved her brother, so she allowed him to keep the Snake People. However, every year they were to hold a council where her rules were to be explained to the young. But time has only deepened the contempt, and now, there is only violence."

I thought about this story. It was familiar and not that far from the readings I had done at the American Philosophical Society as an initiate. "We got a similar story," I said. "Genesis, chapter three, verses fourteen through fifteen, 'And the Lord God said unto the serpent... I will put enmity between thee and the woman, and between thy seed and her seed; it shall bruise thy head, and thou shalt bruise his heel.'"

"Yes, similar." Tecumseh nodded. "But it is in differences that danger lies. These you must see as well."

One of his men at the cooking fire stood up and waved us over.

"Come." Tecumseh extended his hand to me. "Join us for fellowship and a meal. You have heard enough of this talk for now."

Having lost my supper back at the homestead, which seemed an eternity ago, my stomach accepted before my words. "I could eat."

We walked toward the fire and the meal.

"Someday, I would like to meet the great Thomas Jefferson," Tecumseh said.

"You two would make quite a pair."

"How is this?"

"You both talk real good," I said.

If I hadn't been convinced I was a prisoner, I would have had one hell of a time. We ate rabbit and squash that had been baked in the coals. The second peeled like a stewed apple. There was singing, laughing, and dancing. They were about the funniest bunch I'd ever been around. It was well past midnight, and those boys had worn me clean out. I bid them a goodnight and retired to my bedroll where, despite the continued revelry, I fell into a deep, dreamless sleep.

The next morning, I woke up to the smell of stewed rabbit and hominy alongside the sound of birds and the wind moving through the hemlocks. I sat up in my bedroll to see Tecumseh down by a fire stirring our breakfast, but the rest of his boys were gone. I dipped my cup in the pool for a drink of water then sat next to him.

"Where'd everybody go?" I asked.

Tecumseh handed me a wooden bowl of stew he'd pulled from a small copper pot. "They have gone after your Monkey Dog."

"They what?"

He dipped himself a bowl and eased back against a rock. "They have gone after the Monkey Dog."

I put my bowl down and stood, feeling a bit spun up, a little foolish. "How long? Where? I need to get after them."

"Not now." Tecumseh continued to eat. "We have different business."

I leaned toward him. "Now look here, this is my mission. My first mission. I'm to take care of this critter, and I ain't about to let you run over what I've been sent to do."

"Your first mission?" If he was bothered, he didn't show it. "That explains how you are still alive." He put his bowl down and wiped his fingers on his britches. "I have decided to make sure you stay that way."

I stood there trying to figure out what he was saying.

"Please, sit. There is much you still don't know. If you would allow, I would like to help. Your Monkey Dog will be waiting."

The cabin, the dead, and catching that first sight of the Monkey Dog, well, it gave me pause. Even with a pocket full of silver and a belly full of fire, I knew I needed more than what I'd come with, so I sat.

"Help how?" I picked up my bowl.

Tecumseh continued his breakfast. "After you retired, we discussed your presence here. Your duty. Your bravery as you faced the *Ya'kwahe*."

I looked at him.

"It was decided you should go with me to *Chala-ka-tha*, our principle town. There, we will meet with my brother, The Prophet."

I knew about Chillicothe and the Prophet, so I wasn't thrilled with the prospect of seeing either. "If I decline? Respectfully?"

Tecumseh finished his stew. "Then you are free to go, but one of two things will happen. You will either never find the Monkey Dog, or if you do, you will most certainly die."

I knew he was right. "So now what?"

Tecumseh pulled himself up. "Last night, you stood before the *Ya'kwahe*. You fully intended to fight it."

"It's my duty. Why I was sent," I said.

"And that is why I will take you to see my brother."

. . . .

Chala-ka-tha, Indian Territory

I had heard much about the great Shawnee Village Chillicothe, the capitol city where their great leader resided. However, I was not prepared for its majesty. Chillicothe was built on a high bluff over a bend in the Scioto River, arranged around a central plaza dominated by a bark covered Council House. Women worked vast fields of corn, squash, and potatoes. Children ran and played. Chillicothe was broad, vast, and thriving. My mind was taken back to Marietta; muddy, primitive, holding its own against the river on one side and the wilderness on the other. I was reminded that I was in their place and not my own.

Tecumseh was greeted warmly by his people as we walked around the fields and houses toward the main Council House, while I was eyed with suspicion. The men seemed bemused, indifferent, but the women were out right hostile, giving me the skunk eye as they went about their work. The children, well, they didn't hold back. The polite ones yelled at me, and the bold ones spit on me. Both were quickly rebuked by Tecumseh.

"We will meet with my brother," Tecumseh said as a crowd gathered around us. "He is a holy man, so expect him to behave in ways that reflect those idiosyncrasies."

I nodded, nervous. I knew the Prophet by reputation, not a good one either. The open door to the Council House darkened with a human form, and the crowd quieted, slowly disappearing back to their work. I swallowed, wondering if anyone needed help weeding a tater patch or two.

I was a bit disappointed when the man who emerged was squirrely with thin arms. He stooped over a round belly, his right eye gone so he squinted it closed. He stopped just outside the doorway, giving me the meanest look I'd ever seen before he walked toward me, his arms swinging at his sides.

Honestly, I figured he meant to hit me.

Tecumseh stepped between us, putting his hand on The Prophet's chest. "Good morning, brother. I see the day finds you well."

The Prophet looked around Tecumseh, sizing me up with his good eye before he looked up at his brother, who was a good head taller, and growled.

"Brother," Tecumseh said,. "this is my friend Daniel Karshner. He is a *Jaeger*, a Hunter like the *Tipwiwe*."

The Prophet rested his head against Tecumseh's arm, listening.

"We met tracking the *Ya'kwahe*. He also was hunting it. He cornered it in a clearing. Stood bravely against it."

I straightened myself and leaned against my long rifle like I had seen Dan Boone do. I didn't want to make a liar out of Tecumseh, so I tried to look brave.

"Where are your men?" the Prophet asked.

"Just me," I replied.

He narrowed that good eye. "Not you. I will not talk to you." The Prophet looked at Tecumseh.

"They have gone to track the monster. It was frightened. It may have fled to its home," Tecumseh said.

"Why?" The Prophet sized me up again. "Why this one?" He waved his hand like he was shooing a fly.

Tecumseh turned to me. "Tell him."

"Beg your pardon?"

"At the cabin. Tell my brother what you saw."

I thought back to the bodies and the torn-up livestock then swallowed to clear my throat. "The family was in the main room. Arranged—"

"No." Tecumseh raised his hand. "The 'haint,' you called it."

"Oh. I saw an apparition. A tall man dressed in grey. I reckoned him the one who murdered the family I was sent to see."

The Prophet moved past Tecumseh. "Did it speak to you?"

"It did."

"What did it say?"

I looked at Tecumseh. "It said, 'listen.'"

The Prophet clasped his brother's arm. "And he shows courage?"

"Yes. And his eyes are open," Tecumseh said.

"We will sit by the fire." The Prophet turned, stomping back to the Council House.

Tecumseh exhaled as hard as I did. "Let us join him."

The Council House was arranged around low benches on the right side, stacked with corn and wooden containers. On the left, platforms reached to the vaulted ceiling. These seemed to be living quarters. Women peeked out the animal skin curtains then let them fall shut. Vents in the ceiling let light in and smoke out from the equally spaced cooking fires dug into the packed earth floor. We walked to the back where a thick curtain of animal hides hung suspended from the ceiling. The Prophet pushed his way through and between two cedar posts that had been sunk into the ground.

"This is the lodge of the Sacred Fire. Here, we will get answers," Tecumseh said.

I followed him in. It was dark and quiet when the skins closed behind us. The inner chamber walls were lined with skins and wooden screens to keep out sound and light. The Prophet climbed onto a platform that rose five feet off the ground, but Tecumseh took a ladder up and took a seat on his brother's the left side.

"Please. Sit there, on the other side of the fire," Tecumseh said.

I sat on the ground. A fire burned between us in a large rock that looked like a mill stone, hollow in the middle but smooth like it was old.

"My brother has told you about the state of war that exists between our Grandmother and her brother?" The Prophet asked.

"He has."

The Prophet raised his hand. "Don't talk. Don't leave your filthy words in this place."

I bristled and looked at Tecumseh, who stared into the fire.

The Prophet peered at his brother out the side of his good eye. Getting no reaction, he straightened.

"Not long ago, I was given a message from the Creator. To end this war, we must give up our old ways and take up the new ways given to us. In this way, we can defeat the Powers Below and their agents." The Prophet nodded at Tecumseh.

"As you have seen, Daniel," said Tecumseh, "our weapons do not work on these creatures. We must acquire sacred weapons."

"Only the brave can approach this sacred place. Only those chosen by the Creator," the Prophet added.

"Our brother sought these weapons," said Tecumseh. "He was brave."

"Where is he now?" I asked.

The Prophet leaned forward, fists clinched, and Tecumseh put out his hand.

"He did not return." He looked toward the Prophet. "Daniel has a right to ask questions that involve this matter." The Prophet crossed his arms and slouched back, out of the firelight.

"What makes you think I was chosen?" I asked.

From the darkness, the Prophet spoke. "The Creator told me to listen as well."

My prickly nature got the better of my tongue. "Did you?"

There was a howl, and the Prophet jumped to his feet, his face red. He looked down at his brother, who sat stone still. "You will take this person to *Yalakuquakumigigi*. He will bear witness. If he is chosen, take him to the Forbidden Place. Take what is needed. If not, never bring this animal to me again."

Tecumseh jumped from the platform then pulled me up and pushed me toward the door.

"Don't take dogs!" the Prophet screamed.

"I will take the dogs, brother," Tecumseh said over his shoulder.

. . . .

Yalakuquakumigigi

We followed the river north until midday, our way marked by earthen mounds. Two dogs followed behind us. Some of the mounds were covered with tall prairie grass, others with maple trees. All of them were old. Tecumseh walked to the top of a mound, scanned the horizon, then adjusted our path to the next mound. From mound to mound, we continued, finally swinging East to pick up a narrow fork in the river.

It was getting late in the day, and our ambulation had yielded little talk, though my head spun with questions. "What is the *Yala, Yala-kuq, Yal?*"

"The Creation Place." Tecumseh stopped and leaned back against a tree. "*Yalakuquakumigigi,* the Universe. Creation." He opened his arms. "All of this is *Yalakuquakumigigi.*"

"So we're there?"

"Yes." Tecumseh said. "Come see."

I followed him up the river bank where we entered a long, walled road, and the dogs trailed behind.

"This is the Great Way to *Yalakuquakumigigi.*" Tecumseh sounded proud. "Long before our people, the Ancient Ones were here. They were powerful magicians, the first of our grandmother's creations, the first Witnesses. Grandmother created this place and gave us rules. The Ancient Ones built a great model of the universe to explain how to live a good life and be good grandchildren."

The dogs settled nearby.

"But when Motshee Manitou created his own people, there were some who wanted his way. As I said before, sometimes the Dark looks more powerful. It seems beautiful because it is easy.

There is no struggle in Darkness," Tecumseh shrugged. "But there is also no strength."

We followed the road for a few miles, the dogs behind us, the way flat and straight until it ended at a massive earthen enclosure. There was a break in the high wall, and an earthen mound was situated just inside what looked to be an octagon.

"This represents the sky," Tecumseh said. "This opening is our intentions. These mounds are the guardians. As we pass, we must acknowledge this truth."

We swung left toward a bottle neck in the earthwork that formed a narrow alley connecting the octagon to an equally impressive circle. Once we entered the circle, Tecumseh spoke again.

"That was the Sky Road, what you call the Milky Way. That is how the Powers Above travel between their world and ours. One day, we will all take that road to the sky. This circle represents the earth."

We cut across the circle that took up some twenty acres. At the far end, facing the Sky Road, stood a conical mound. Tecumseh, hurried as the day faded, pointed to an earthen crown work that extended from the mound.

"You will wait here."

I sat while Tecumseh built a small fire, and the dogs sat just outside the firelight. He took a leather bag from his pack, opening it to reveal an effigy pipe of a horned man that he filled.

"This is a powerful truth bearer. Smoke it. It will call the Creator to you," he said.

"What is it?"

"*Kinnikinnick*, a sacred mixture. Do not fear it. It will help you." He handed me the pipe. "The dogs will protect you. They are guides. Trust them. They will only allow what is needed. This is a powerful thing to know."

"Wait," I said when he stood. "Where're you going?"

"Away. This is not for me. I will camp where we came in. Find me once it has found you."

"What's coming?" I fretted.

"Good luck, Daniel."

. . . .

I took a long pull on the pipe and felt the smoke burn into my lungs as the dogs settled at my feet. I looked northeast, across the circle toward the sky road. Night had fallen heavily. It was harder to see, and the guardian mound slowly receded into the darkness.

There was a light. Dim at first, then flashing. I thought it Tecumseh with a torch, headed my way. I started to stand, ready for this foolishness to be over, but the tobacco played funny with me. I fell back against the earthen cradle, and the dogs whined, putting their paws on my legs. The flashing light shot up orange then hung in the sky, burning, spinning, getting brighter until I had to shade my eyes, putting me in mind of the firework rockets I'd seen at an Independence Day celebration in Philadelphia.

This rocket didn't explode. It simply opened, a window of daytime in the night sky. I closed my eyes and shook my head then, with one eye, took a careful glance. The gray haint was there in the sky, standing in the center of the circle. He held a staff in one hand and a lantern in the other.

"*Hwaet*," he said. I looked up to see him staring hard at me from under his hat. "Remember."

The hole shrunk to nothing as a red comet fell from the sky and smashed into the center of the circle. I shielded my eyes but felt no heat, so I peeked over my hand to see a fire burning at the place of impact. A serpent with thick human arms pulled itself from the ground. Wings grew from its narrow back. It locked eyes on me and crawled my way, but when I tried to move, my body was frozen.

There was lightning followed by the loudest thunder I'd ever heard, and I realized I was screaming. A golden man fell from the sky, a scale in one hand and a sword in his other. He ran the sword through the throat of that serpent, and there was quiet.

Then the fire became a sea.

I saw a big man, his hair and braided beard red, sailing in a boat. A great, green serpent with yellow eyes rose from the water to tower over him. The man roared and stretched himself up, his back a rack of muscle like a bull's. He raised a glowing hammer over his head and swung it at the serpent, hitting it with the sound of thunder as the serpent fell back.

But the man was soon gone, and the serpent was still. A little fellow crawled out of a hole in the ground to look at the serpent. He took a long hunting knife from a scabbard and plunged it into the critter, digging around until he pulled out the heart. Then he turned to me and...

He turned right into another man. This one wasn't like the others. He was old, alone, tired. He raised a shield and pulled his body behind it, raising a sword over his head. Another serpent dropped from the sky, breathing fire, but the old man stood firm even as fire washed over him. He came around with the sword, taking a swipe at the monster. The sword struck, but the beast sank its teeth into the man. He yelled and hacked at that writhing beast.

Then it was quiet.

I was alone again except for the dogs, who both lay on my chest. The pipe was still in my hand. The circle was just as before— open, quiet, and untouched.

· · · · · · · · · ●●●●●●● · · · · · · · · · ·

I relayed what I'd seen to Tecumseh, who listened with stern determination. "We must go to the Forbidden Place," he said.

Forbidden was all I needed to hear. "Or we can take the name for what it is."

"Your vision says we must continue." He pulled the blanket over himself and rolled to his side. "Sleep. The dogs will leave when you do."

· ·

The Forbidden Place

For two days, we followed the woods to a steep slope that twisted itself up to the curve of a hill. It summited to a terrace about two hundred feet wide, dotted with more ancient earth works. A mound, maybe ten feet tall, stood in front of us, and a long earthen wall ran down the center of the table land. Tecumseh breathed deep, gulping. The place had a feeling that seeped through my leggings and crept up under my britches, and the air crackled like when lightning hits too close.

"Come here and see," said Tecumseh.

I followed him up the mound to a platform where I sucked in my breath. Stretched along the table land was the effigy of a long, undulating snake. Its form rose some five feet above the surface and wound a thousand feet north. To my left, I could see its triple-coiled tail. Far off, the body ended in a head, two horns protruding from the sides. It looked to be biting at a large oval, perhaps an egg.

"Holy Hell," I muttered.

"This is the story. Can you read it?" he asked.

I tried to take the whole earthen critter in. It was meaningful but unintelligible to me. "No, sir. I can't."

Tecumseh looked over the serpent. "This says the story too. Our uncle created the Great Serpents. They nurse a grudge against human beings. There are two kinds. Of them, the *Ukteni*, the Horned Serpent, is greater. These are the most powerful of all the monsters, seldom seen but always in the world through the Sorcerers who do their work. Then there is the lesser serpent, the Horse-Headed Snake. These are what your people call dragons. You saw both in your vision."

Dragons. Yes, but... "Why is this a forbidden place?"

"Long ago, the war between our Grandmother and her brother spilled over into our world. The Serpents took their grievances to the Ancient Ones, attacking them, killing many. They tried to fight back, but, as you have seen, our weapons are useless against these powers. So Grandmother sent her army, the Thunderbirds."

He took in a deep breath. "The two powers met here, and a battle was fought. The Thunderbirds defeated the *Ukteni* but at a great cost. Their powerful weapons, thunder, lightning, and wind set fire to the earth. A great flood was sent to quell the fire, and many of the Ancient Ones died. Some lived, and they became our teachers. Others aligned with Motshee Manitou, and that war continues among proxies."

I rubbed at my beard, as thoughtful as I was nervous. "What's here for us?"

"Your vision recalled your people's memory of this war. It calls us back to where the battle occurred. The key to defeating the Powers Below lies at the Forbidden Place. Like any battlefield, the fallen left weapons. We were told, so very long ago, that in the crater left by the battle, we would find the tools to defeat the Powers Below."

"Why not just go if you know it's here?"

"Many have gone. None have returned. The place is guarded by the Horse-Headed Snakes. They are formidable."

"Why me? Why us?" I asked.

"We have always known that somewhere, someone had the key to defeating the Horse-Headed Snakes. Your vision recalls that your people knew how throughout time."

"They might've." My blood ran cold with a hard truth. "But I got no idea."

Tecumseh started down the mound. "You must remember, or we will both die." I looked at Tecumseh to see he wasn't fooling. "We must try." We headed north along the hilltop, me numb behind him.

"What happened to everyone? The ones who took care of this place?" I finally asked.

"They're dead, Below, and the Horse-Headed Snakes rule them. The Teachers maintained this place as a boundary between the powers. The truce held for a long time. Both sides feared the wrath of the Thunderbirds."

"What upset the truce?"

Tecumseh stopped and faced me. "Your people. The Powers Below did not consider you a part of the truce. They kill you. You kill us. We fight you. We fight them. We all die but them. The evil ones thrive in the fog of chaos."

I opened my mouth to speak, but I was at a loss.

"So the Horse-Headed Snakes rose up to kill the Teachers. They started a war that will kill us all," he said.

"So we get the weapons and stop them?"

"Others have promised the same. I hope we fare better."

We reached the oval and skirted around the edge of the cliff that dropped to the bottoms. The wide flat plane accommodated three small tributaries that fed a wide, swift moving creek cutting through the forest. I was looking at a meteor crater, I realized, and my heart dropped as I wondered what kind of weapons Tecumseh hoped to find.

"Here," he said. "This is the delta where only grass grows. It is where we will find what we have come for." I looked at him, uncertain. "We must be vigilant," he continued. "This is where it begins or ends for us all."

"That's not an encouraging speech," I told him.

"Then I will work on my oratory."

"Aristotle's a good start," I said. "Shakespeare ain't bad either."

"I hope to read them soon."

We started down a riprapped switchback that wound to a series of natural terraces, to the bottoms where Tecumseh dropped his gear and took out two shovels. "Start digging."

I had no clue what we were looking for, but after a few minutes of frenzied digging, Tecumseh whooped and laid a flat rock on a deer hide he'd spread on the ground between us. "This is it, Daniel. This is what we have come for."

I went over for a look. "Meteoric iron."

Tecumseh was breathless. "Yes, this is it. But we must find more. Dig."

I went to pulling up chunks of meteor and tossing them on the deerskin. We'd amassed quite a pile when my ears started ringing. I shook my head, sniffing, smelling something like a full privy after a hard rain followed by cucumber. I looked back, toward the run we'd crossed, and there it stood.

When Tecumseh said Horse-Headed Snake, I took him to be speaking figuratively, but it was as thick as a man and some twenty feet long, all muscle and meanness. Its head was long and thick, just like a horse, even to the mane. I saw no ears, but they could have been laid against its head, and the thing looked as mad as a hornet knocked into a water bucket.

It wrapped itself around a dead tree while I stood there with my mouth hanging open like a fool, too shocked to be scared and too dumb to run.

Tecumseh raised his long gun, and the Horse-Headed Snake reared up to look down on us. Its eyes were white, but they turned a milky blue then flashed red. It tossed its head back, hissing and heaving, almost like it was laughing.

There was the muted sound of flint striking steel when Tecumseh squeezed the trigger, signaling a misfire. He dropped his rifle and pulled his knife and tomahawk from his belt.

Then...

I remembered. I pushed Tecumseh out of the way and pulled my shovel up, pointing the handle at the critter like a long gun. It stopped like it hadn't noticed me before. Its eyes...white to blue to red then it tossed its head back to laugh. I dropped that shovel and pulled my pistols, firing both, sending two .50 caliber balls to where the head tapered into the body. It looked at me as if it was surprised and collapsed to the ground.

Tecumseh fell on it, hacking at the neck, taking off the head. The critter's horse face lay there looking at us with dead eyes while the body twisted in a prolonged death dance.

"I remembered," I said. "A snake'll hex your weapon. When Pa and Granddad walked the fence line, my granddad would take a walking stick, my pa a blunderbuss. When they come on a snake, Granddad would point the walking stick like it was a rifle. The snake would hex it, and Pa would take the shot."

Tecumseh started laughing. I'd yet to hear his laugh, and it was such a good noise that I joined him.

"Here you've been teaching me how to stay alive," I said. "Come to find out, there's a couple few things I can learn you."

"Yes. Just as I had hoped," said Tecumseh. "Let us finish here before another comes to test us."

. . . .

Chala-ka-tha

In Chillicothe, we set to work turning those iron meteorites into weapons. I worked at heating the stone, pulling out the metal and hammering it into shape. I let the metal speak to me, and before long, I had worked a bearded axe head that I honed to a shaving edge. I was happy with it, but it still needed a handle.

This was a weapon of the sky. It needed a handle that recalled the Powers Above.

I studied on it a minute, deciding that it needed an Oak handle. In the stories I'd heard as a boy, the sky gods favored oak.

"There is an oak tree just over there." Tecumseh pointed. "It was struck by lightning last spring."

"That'll do just fine." I cut a thick branch and fashioned a handle that could be swung with either hand then I wrapped it in soft deerskin, making a right proper weapon if I do say so.

Tecumseh worked alongside me, smithing a nasty-looking blade that he affixed to a gunstock club. Into the hickory, he carved a representation of the serpent earthwork where we had collected the iron. "A reminder of the lesson you taught us." He swung his weapon with satisfaction.

I felt right proud.

The old man with the scar I'd first met, the one who'd dismissed me, Blackfish was his name, was working with two of his men to make iron arrow heads. We aimed to be a formidable force.

Tecumseh came to where I sat with Blackfish. "He and his warriors returned the day before we arrived. They followed your Monkey Dog and have found the village of the Sorcerers."

I nodded, ready for what might come next.

"Tomorrow, we will go there, and for the first time, take this war to them." But Tecumseh seemed worried.

"This'll work all right."

"It has been a long time of promises and stories, and there's been much suffering in between. I am hesitant to be optimistic."

I don't know what I expected; I reckon some kind of big war dance, but once we had armed ourselves, Blackfish's warriors left to scout ahead while Blackfish went to his wigwam to get a few hours of sleep. Tecumseh told me I should do the same, offering me a lean-to next to a pleasant little creek that made some fine music while he went to the Council House to confer with his brother. As I drifted to sleep, I could only wonder what words passed between them.

. . . .

Indian Territory

We were up before dawn, me, Tecumseh, and Blackfish starting toward the Sorcerer's town. The industrious optimism from the day before was gone, and my mouth was dry with fear. I'd faced that critter once, fired on it, intended to chase it into the night. That had been just a week ago. Now I was wondering if I shouldn't have turned tail and run when that haint first got the drop on me back at the farm.

"You are smarter now," Tecumseh said.

"How's that?"

"Ignorance is its own kind of bravery. Knowledge is strategy. You must apply it just as ignorance asks that you ignore your better judgement."

"I reckon you can read minds, then?" I said.

"No. It is all in your face." Tecumseh patted my back. "You should never play cards, my friend."

Blackfish chuckled.

"I don't like cards," I said, and he chuckled harder.

About noon, we caught up with two of Blackfish's men who'd gone out ahead. I couldn't understand what they were saying, but they were spun up by what they'd seen.

Tecumseh was grim. "This morning, the Sorcerers left their village. They'd received word, no doubt, that we had defeated their Snake Horse."

"Damn it to Hell." I'd spent the better part of the ambulation getting myself set. I was as ready now as I'd ever be and possibly never be again.

"They left three *Ya'kwahe* in the village to prevent our pursuit," said Tecumseh. "Even if the Sorcerers elude us for now, these creatures must be dealt with."

I touched my axe. "Well, let's get to it."

We crawled through a tangle of underbrush to an overhang that looked down into a village arranged around a central plaza where a small fire smoked itself out in the dampness. Dug out wigwams topped with fallen trees and prairie grass were scattered around the plaza. If it hadn't been for the fire, it would have looked like a clearing in the forest. Pacing the perimeter were three Monkey Dogs, mean, angry, and ready.

"They are waiting for us," Tecumseh said.

We moved back from the overhang.

"You will stay here," Tecumseh told Blackfish. "Give us time to approach the village then fire on the creatures. Daniel and I will attack from below. If we fail, kill us. Do not allow us to be turned."

"How's that?" I stared at him.

Tecumseh put his hand on my shoulder. "It is time to test our stories."

The sky rumbled and the rain started. We made our way to the village on our bellies, keeping to a narrow run-off that was slowly filling with water. We reached the forest floor, and the Monkey Dogs came into sight as the rain fell unimpeded.

Tecumseh smiled. "The Powers Above bless us."

I pulled the axe from my belt, my wet hands firm on the wrapped handle.

Over the rain and thunder, we heard one of the Monkey Dogs rear up with a hellacious scream. Three arrows stuck from its back like spikes, and it dropped to the muddy plaza.

There wasn't much ground between us and the remaining two Monkey Dogs, so we ran at them, Tecumseh and I hollering something frightful. I didn't even know I could make such a sound.

I lost Tecumseh as the booger closest to me raised its massive arm to swipe at me, so I took a one-handed swing with my axe across the Monkey Dog's belly, opening that critter clean up, its guts spilling like pink soup beans from a torn poke.

That critter looked at me like it couldn't believe what I'd done then dropped to all fours, shuffled backed, and reared up again. I grabbed my axe with both hands to finish it.

Tecumseh rose by my side to drive his club deep into the Monkey Dog's chest. It stumbled, dropping on its thick, dirty forearms as it looked at me. I'd never seen its eyes, being as they were either too far away or covered by a thick brow ridge, but it had human eyes. Sad. Trapped. Scared. Then it struggled its giant body up on those thick hindquarters, moaning as Tecumseh worked to free his war club from the booger's chest. I swung my axe hard and took that critter's head clean off, so it bounced across the plaza. The critter dropped, and the only sounds were rain and a far rumble of thunder.

Tecumseh let loose a shout that ran through the trees. I could hear Blackfish and his boys up behind me yelling too, but I was lost. My heart was beating fast, and I felt like running. I took an uncertain step and dropped to my knees. The other Monkey Dog was dead, three arrows, nicely grouped, in its chest, its throat laid open by Tecumseh's war club. I remember the mud as being the only thing natural about that moment, and damn it, if I didn't cry.

Tecumseh greeted Blackfish and the archers with loud talk, and I stood after a moment, trying to smile.

"We did it!" Tecumseh said. "You did it, Daniel! We have the weapons to fight this war and will not be victims of this evil."

I wiped my nose with my sleeve. "The Sorcerers are still out there, probably looking for their next victims to turn into these. We should hold off celebrating till we take care of those fellows."

Blackfish nodded.

"You are right." Tecumseh's smile tightened. "We must stop them before they can do more."

"But what about these?" I said, looking at the Monkey Dog dead in the plaza.

Tecumseh studied me. "What about them?"

"You said they were human once. This wasn't their choice. I reckon they deserve a burial is all."

Tecumseh looked at me fitful, but Blackfish turned to his boys.

"They were our people first, before they were taken. They return to us now. Daniel's right."

The bodies proved too heavy to move, and we had no tools to dig, but one of the archers found dry wood in a Sorcerer's wigwam. The rain had moved ahead of us, and we had enough wood to get three pyres going. I understood Tecumseh's impatience, but there was still work to be done.

We picked up the Sorcerer's trail in the forest. Despite the very recent victory, there was no talk. I feared I'd soured the day with my desire to honor the humans in them poor critters, but I wasn't sorry.

There was a rush overhead, like wind but only in the highest part of the trees, then thunder. We stopped walking as darkness folded around us. Blackfish and his boys dropped to their knees, their faces buried in the mud as Tecumseh put his hand on my shoulder.

"There."

Up ahead, where the forest dipped into a deep creek bed and rose back up, stood a figure. It had the shape of a man, and I went for my axe.

Tecumseh put his hand on my arm. "No."

I looked at him and back to the figure. It was tall, maybe seven feet, but the lay of the land could have been playing funny with my perspective, and my eyes weren't adjusted to the dark. The thing seemed to have no head, just high rounded shoulders.

Then, from what I reckoned was its chest, red circles appeared. They sparkled and crackled like crimson lightning.

Tecumseh dropped to his knees and tried to pull me down, but I was mesmerized by the creature's eyes, which twirled and glowed. The figure relaxed its shoulders, and a set of enormous wings stretched from its back. That's when I didn't so much as take a knee as drop from fright, landing beside Tecumseh.

Its scream went in my ears to shake my whole body, radiating down my spine to my toes. All was quiet. The figure was gone and the darkness with it.

Blackfish stood and turned around, walking quickly past us, his archers in tow.

"What the Hell was that?" I cried at Tecumseh.

"That was a Thunderbird. We are done, for now." He turned and started back down the trail toward his home.

. . . .

Chala-ka-tha, **Indian Territory**

I loaded my borrowed canoe with supplies for the trip back to Marietta. Blackfish handed me a pack of dried meat and for the first time, a smile. "Bring back the canoe. I don't want to come after you."

"Agreed," I told him, and we shook hands.

I watched him walk up the trail toward Chillicothe then took a look at the Council House where the Prophet kept himself. I hadn't had his company since our first meeting, and I couldn't say I was sorry, but my thoughts changed when Tecumseh started down the path toward me. I reminded myself to practice his walk. It brought a confidence that told the world to get out of your way.

"My brother still nurses a grudge toward you," Tecumseh s

aid, and I was more certain than ever that he could read my thoughts.

"Well, that hurts some, I reckon."

Tecumseh studied my packed canoe before he next spoke. "My brother has struggled to find his role among us. Such is the life for one who has his body in this world and his mind in another. He has spent his time as a leader teaching the people to let go of the white ways, that what will save us is a return to the ways of the Shawnee." He paused. "And now there is you."

"Didn't mean no disrespect. I had a job to do and was fixed to do it."

"I am glad you did," Tecumseh said. "Because of you, we know how to defeat the Serpents. We can now make weapons to fight the Sorcerers and their army. We are thankful for your presence and your teaching."

"I'm grateful for your teaching too. It pains me to say it, but I almost feel like those folks in Philadelphia were fixed on getting me killed."

Tecumseh plucked a dandelion from a patch of green by the river and held it up.

"This flower," he said. "It was unknown to my great grandfather, yet my son will always know it. Your people brought this to us. Like you, it should not be rooted in this land, but here it is. Once we listened, we benefitted from its wisdom. Our honey is sweeter. This flower is good for food and medicine." He handed the dandelion to me. "It must be this way with us as well. We have much to share with each other. Since the beginning of time, this war between light and darkness has been fought, and darkness tries to feed on our divide and conquer ways. Yet here we are, together. We could end this war in our time, if we are wise."

I admired his optimism. "I'll share this with Mr. Jefferson. I think he'll agree."

Tecumseh shook my hand. "One more thing." He handed me a small brown nut on a sinew cord that I held up to admire.

"It's a buckeye, called so because it resembles the eye of a deer, always alert for danger. It is for protection."

I put it around my neck. "Thank ye."

Tecumseh nodded. "And thank you."

I stood at my canoe as I watched Tecumseh fade into the landscape. We'd see each other again, I was certain of it. I set my canoe and let the current take me away from Chillicothe, confident that he and I would face many more perils as friends.

Mountain Gap Books sincerely hopes you enjoyed reading this book as much as we did. If so, we would greatly appreciate a short review on your favorite book website. Reviews are crucial for any author, and even just a line or two can make a huge difference.

About the Authors in

Haints and Hollers

By Order of Their First Appearance

Deborah Marshall: "Messages"

Deborah, commonly known is Debbie, began her life in Johnson City, Tennessee. Before she turned one, her family moved to Letcher County, Kentucky, where she spent the majority of her childhood. As an adult, she moved to Greenville, South Carolina, where she became a nurse and practiced until retirement. She has two living children, Keith and Mandy, and one deceased son, John. She has grandchildren and a great grandchild. Like many Appalachians, she married young. "Messages" is her first foray into published fiction.

....

Rebecca Lynn: "Can Johnny Come Home with us?"

Rebecca Lynn met and married her college sweetheart while he was in the Marine Corps, and together they raised their three children in upstate New York. Lynn published articles in psychology and short fiction pieces before becoming a member of the Romance Writers of America. She is no stranger to the supernatural and has many chilling tales to share.

Website: AskRebeccaLynn.wordpress.com
Instagram: @AuthorRebeccaLynn

....

Brenda G'Fellers: "Miss Vera," "Strays," "Survival"

Brenda G'Fellers has worked as a teacher, school librarian and school administrator, instructional coach, and a college professor and is currently working as a public librarian. Aside from some professional articles, her first published book, a children's biography, was published in 2018. She is at work on another children's biography and is pleased to share these short stories.

A native of Appalachia, Brenda has two daughters and three grandchildren. She and her husband make their home in Tennessee.

Publications
– *Rhea Wells; Boy of Jonesborough*. Mountain Gap Books. 2018.

....

Jeanne G'Fellers: "A Visit from a Peculiar Entity," "The Neighbors are Fantastic," "Great Uncle's Rocking Chair"

Born and raised in the foothills of the Appalachian Mountains, award-winning Science Fiction and Fantasy author Jeanne G'Fellers' early memories include watching the original *Star Trek* series with their father and reading the stacks of books their librarian mother brought home. Jeanne's influences include authors Anne McCaffrey, Ursula K. LeGuin, Octavia Butler, Isaac Asimov, and Frank Herbert.

Jeanne lives in Northeast Tennessee with their spouse and an assortment of crazy felines. Their home is tucked against a small woodland where they regularly see wildlife and experience the magic of the natural world.

Author website: jeannegfellersauthor.com
Twitter: twitter.com/jlgfellers
Facebook Author Page: facebook.com/Jeannegfellersauthor
Author Instagram: instagram.com/authorjeannegfellers/

Publications
The Appalachian Elementals Series
 – *Cleaning House* (Mountain Gap Books) #1
 – *Keeping House* (Mountain Gap Books) #2
Appalachian Elementals Side Tales
 – *Mama, Me, and the Holiday Tree* (Mountain Gap Books)
 – *Striking Balance* (Mountain Gap Books, 2020)
The Surrogate Series
 – *Surrogate* (Supposed Crimes Publisher)
 – *Surrogate: Hunted* (Supposed Crimes Publisher)
 – *Surrogate: Traditions* (Upcoming from Mountain Gap Books)
The Sisters Series (Bella Books)
 – *No Sister of Mine*
 – *Sister Lost Sister Found*
 – *Sisters Flight*
 – *No Sisters Keeper*

....

Sarah Elizabeth: "Singin' Sally"

Sarah Elizabeth is an emerging writer in Johnson City, Tennessee, with several published pieces and is a contributing writer for *The Yarn Exchange Radio Show* on WETS, East Tennessee State University's student-run radio station.

Publications
Sarah Elizabeth has been published in *World Poetry Library*, *Sojourn*; and has won the Purple Crayon Writing Contest.

....

Jules Corriere: "Born with a Veil"

Jules Corriere has been a playwright and theater director for twenty years, creating plays from oral stories found within communities that bring people together over divides of age, culture, religion, politics, and other barriers. Her work has been performed at the Kennedy Center. She's received the Presidential Points of Light Award and has toured England, Scotland, and Brazil. She currently writes the monthly storytelling radio show, "A Night with the Yarn Exchange," which is in its eighth season.

Author website: julescorriere.com

Publications
   – *Story Bridge: From Alienation to Community Action.* (with Richard Owen Geer)

....

Anne G'Fellers-Mason: "Pieces and Parts," "Causing a Scene"

Anne G'Fellers-Mason lives in Jonesborough in a family compound with her spouse and crazy cats. She grew up in Northeast Tennessee and currently works to preserve and interpret the region's history at the Heritage Alliance. She has a BA in Theatre/History, an MA in History, and an MFA in Playwriting. She gets to combine her passions through her local history-based plays. Her first novel, *The Summer Between*, was published in October of 2018.

Author website: annegfellersmasonauthor.com
Twitter: twitter.com/anne_fellers
Facebook Author Page: facebook.com/annegfellersmason

Publications
Novels:
– *The Summer Between* (Mountain Gap Books)
– *Flying Upon One Wing* (Coming 2020 from Mountain Gap Books)

Plays
– "The Dance We Do" included as part of *Great Expectations: Eight Short Plays About Teens Under Pressure*, published by YouthPLAYS
– "You, Me, and Alice" included as part of *A Mourning Hollow*, published by Polychoron Press
– "One Last Trick" included as part of *Please Say Yes: Short Plays About Promposing*, published by YouthPLAYS

Kristin Pearson: "As Light Fades"

Kristin Pearson spends her days answering reference and genealogy questions at a public library. She grew up in the flat cornfields of Indiana but has deep and complicated family roots in the coal mines of Kentucky. She and her husband live in northeast Tennessee along with four cats and occasionally a college student daughter or two. This is her first publication.

....

Edward Karshner: "The Salt Creek Valley Monkey Dog"

Edward Karshner was born in Ross County, Ohio, and grew up in the Salt Creek Valley of Southeast Appalachia Ohio, which draws together Ross, Hocking, and Pickaway Counties. He researches and writes about Appalachian folklore, magic, and mysticism. Karshner enjoys autumn in the Hocking Hills, Chillicothe Paints baseball, and the Circleville Pumpkin Show. He lives in Oberlin, Ohio with his wife, Kim, their children, James and Alexandria, and a mixed breed dog named Carlos.

– "These Stories Sustain Me: The Wyrd-ness of My Appalachia," in *Appalachian Reckoning: A Region Responds to* Hillbilly Elegy. Anthony Harkins and Meredith McCarroll, editors. West Virginia University Press, 2019.
– "In the Fullness of Time" (guest writer). *The Blind Pig and the Acorn: A Blog of Appalachian Folklore, Food, Language, and Music.* May 7, 2019. www.blindpigandtheacorn.com/in-the-fullness-of-time

Mountain Gap Books 2019

Printed in the USA
CPSIA information can be obtained
at www.ICGtesting.com
LVHW091158271023
762201LV00004B/757

9 781732 327788